*Total-E-Bound Publishing books from Sedonia Guillone:*

# TOUCHING FOREVER

SEDONIA GUILLONE

Touching Forever
ISBN # 978-1-907280-82-5
©Copyright Sedonia Guillone 2010
Cover Art by Lyn Taylor ©Copyright 2009
Interior text design by Claire Siemaszkiewicz
Total-E-Bound Publishing

Published in 2010 by Total-E-Bound Publishing  Faldingworth Road, Spridlington, Market Rasen, Lincolnshire, LN8 2DE, UK.

# TOUCHING FOREVER

# Dedication

To Mitch, always.

# Prologue

*Women, the goddesses of Heaven, seek to descend toward Earth to acquire the* yang *essences of males to maintain their goddess position, as men seek to ascend upward to Heaven from Earth to attain the* yin *essence of females to become gods.*
~Madame Lin from *The White Tigress Manual*

*Tibet, A.D. 900*

A shadow covered the mouth of the cave.

Tenzin registered the increase of darkness through his closed eyelids. The presence of a physical body muffled the whistling of the winds around the rocks outside, and from the depths of his meditation, which left him at rest and vibrantly attentive at the same time, his awareness expanded to include the stranger's distress.

No, not distress exactly. Need. Hunger.

The stranger's footsteps scraped, one by one, across the stone floor, making the scratch of pebbles echo through the still depths of the cave.

Tenzin did not break his lotus posture or open his eyes, for his absorption in the mantra made movement and speech difficult. Only when the footsteps stopped directly in front of him did Tenzin drag up his eyelids.

The visitor was breathing raggedly. Flakes of snow clung to his shaggy dark hair, eyelashes, and heavy beard stubble. His tall form emanated physical strength, its broadness hidden by layers of heavy clothing. He dropped to his knees, bringing his gaze even to Tenzin's.

Tenzin stared. Spirals of fear whispered through his body. Never before had he seen a pair of eyes glow like those of the man before him.

The man's ruggedly strong facial features showed he was from a different part of the world. His eyes, gleaming like tiny lanterns, were large and round. Thick raven hair rioted about his face and jaw, matching the heavy stubble on his cheeks. His skin, a swarthy reddish colour, also had a strange glow about it.

Tenzin's heartbeat rose. No normal man's eyes would appear like this. Tibetan culture was rich in demon lore. Could this possibly be the legendary son of the *brag srin mo*, the ogress of the hills? The creature was a myth, supposedly, but in this wild land of snows, anything could lurk, unseen indefinitely by the human eye. This demon son was said to crave human flesh and blood as its food. Which meant that the lust in those glowing eyes was bloodlust...

Remaining in his lotus posture, Tenzin tried to imagine what Lord Buddha would have done if confronted with a demon such as this. In truth, the Buddha had faced many demons by understanding their emptiness. Those, however, had been his inner demons, apparitions which he'd learned had no substance other than what the power of his mind gave them.

The being in front of him, on the other hand, was quite real. Of flesh and blood, judging by the feral scent radiating off his skin and clothing, barely masked by the incense Tenzin had lit before meditation. Facing such a…man…as this, with eyes glowing, hunger palpable… Tenzin had no example on which to draw, no one to help him.

He was truly, utterly alone.

"I am a simple monk," he managed to say. His voice mingled with the panting breath of the stranger. "I have nothing to offer but a cup of yak butter tea and my company in this wild land." Tenzin swallowed hard, his throat suddenly dry and tight.

The man remained silent. He curled back his upper lip to reveal a pair of gleaming fangs, their smooth, sharp whiteness like that of a snow leopard's incisors.

Tenzin refused to break his posture, refused to run. He came from a strong people, people whose strength was compassion, not violence. He had no defence against a creature like this, whose hunger would probably drive him to take Tenzin's life. As a monk who'd devoted all of his four and thirty years to prayer and meditation, he would die with dignity, face the death for which he'd been preparing since birth.

He made his choice none too soon.

The stranger grabbed his shoulders, his grip powerful, inescapable. The pressure of his hands rooted Tenzin down on his hassock. The man-creature leant towards him, his lips curled back, fangs flashing in the lantern glow.

The demon's hot breath pulsed across the side of Tenzin's neck, just before he licked the supple skin. The sensation was surprisingly pleasant. A groan vibrated in the demon's throat. The sound trilled against Tenzin's skin, and his body tingled in a sensuous way that, though he tried to fight it, aroused him, made his body want what was happening to him.

A sudden prick of pain made Tenzin jolt. His breath hitched as the fangs sank into his skin. He groaned softly as pleasure invaded his body, swirling with icy heat in his gut and down into his cock. His eyelids fluttered, and then all the tension in his body ran out like water in a stream.

The demon slid his fangs out. Tenzin sighed and tilted his head a bit more as soft lips closed over the wound. The sensation was intensely pleasurable, like the eruption of seed from his male stem. As a monk, he'd foregone the pleasure of women but had used his own hand, enough to know…

Tenzin's mind relaxed, emptied of thought in the way he'd striven for in meditation. The crags of the cave's interior, cast in shadows by the lantern light, now blurred in his vision, and he heard only the whistle of the winds outside and the murmurs of satisfaction as the demon drank his blood.

Tenzin moaned. Pleasure now spread to every part of his body, covered the surface of his skin, made him tingle right to the tips of his fingers and toes. His vision went out of focus, and his own heartbeat now crashed in his ears, each pulse punctuated by the ecstatic suction of the demon's lips.

Moment by moment, Tenzin's heartbeat slowed. Beat by beat, he heard the decreased rhythm, and the world around him began to fade. His vision grew darker and his body sagged like a limp doll in the demon's iron grip.

The demon lifted his lips away from Tenzin's neck and looked at him. The creature's eyes still glowed, and droplets of blood clung to his lips. The demon leaned into Tenzin again and licked the punctures. The moist warmth against the tiny wounds sent more waves of unfathomable pleasure through Tenzin's body.

Tenzin groaned again. His *likpa* was fully erect under his monk's robes, in spite of his weakened state. His eyelids fluttered; his head tilted back. And then the world went black.

\* \* \* \*

Tenzin opened his eyes. His mind and body felt as if they were floating. He blinked, becoming aware of the shadows flickering on the cave walls. As consciousness seeped into his body, he opened his mouth, only to find his tongue stuck to the roof of his mouth by terrible, sticky dryness. A low rumble vibrated in his ears.

"The sound you hear is your own hunger."

Tenzin blinked again. The voice spoke in his language. In the shadows, a face appeared, hovering over him. *The demon.* He looked more like a man now. His eyes no longer glowed but were a deep brown.

"You'll be all right." The stranger knelt by his side. He held up a bag made of skins. "All I could find for you was some sheep-like animal. Until you learn to feed, this creature's blood will have to do." His voice was deep, smooth, and he spoke Tibetan as easily as if it were his own language.

*No. No blood.* Tenzin tried to say the words out loud, but the dryness enabled him only to make a guttural sound, like a beast. Since taking his vows, he'd not eaten any meat, and now this stranger was about to feed him blood.

"I know your holy people do not eat flesh," the demon said as if he'd heard Tenzin's thoughts, "but you are no longer one of them." He brought the sack of blood closer to Tenzin's face.

*I will not drink that.* Tenzin eyed the sack and shrank back as much as his strength would allow.

"I'm afraid you have no choice. Blood is the food of the undead."

Tenzin looked up. The demon seemed to have read his mind.

The demon grinned. "Yes, I can read your thoughts now."

Before Tenzin could answer, the man-creature opened the top of the skin, and the scent of blood filled the air — coppery, sweet, pungent. To his horror, Tenzin's mouth began to water. Craving, wild, unfettered, as deep and vital as the sexual drive he'd worked so hard to overcome, now grasped him.

He reached up and snatched the skin sack from the stranger's hands.

The stranger didn't hold it back from him, but instead cradled Tenzin's head, lifting him gently, and put the opening of the skin to Tenzin's lips. He tilted the skin so Tenzin could drink. Tenzin pulled the man's hand closer, closing his lips over the opening of the skin.

*Ahhh.* He gulped down the warm liquid, as thick as syrup, unable to satisfy his desire until he'd drunk so much he had to pause for breath. He stopped only long enough to pant a few times, then grasped for the sack once more.

The stranger smiled at him. His dark eyes nearly glowed again. "We have eternity together, you and I, my friend." The voice caressed Tenzin even as the demon's fingertips ran gently down his temple. "I will show you *every* pleasure that existence has to offer."

Tenzin drained the last of the blood from the skin, panting now from the ravenous way he'd drunk the blood. Mortification gripped him. What manner of creature had this demon made of him?

The demon passed a hand over Tenzin's brow. "I see you are disgusted by your enjoyment of blood. Don't worry; you'll grow to accept that part of you just as you'll come to crave my touch." He slid his fingertips down Tenzin's cheek and brushed them across the seam of his lips.

Tenzin shut his eyes and steeled himself against the creature's soft touch. The mere whisper of those fingertips on his skin made his *likpa* throb with need. *Lord Buddha, help me!* he prayed silently and then called up his mantra, which rose and repeated in his mind, like a beacon through the darkness of lust.

"No one can help you now, my love," the demon said. "Not even your gods."

Tenzin gritted his teeth against the demon's arrogance and steeled his resolve not to become like this creature. "I am not yours," he ground out. He wanted to rise, to run from the cave, back to the haven of his monastery, but the demon's touch held him prisoner.

The demon leaned over and slid his touch down Tenzin's throat, and down, to his collarbone. Back and forth, he brushed his fingertips, like the touch of a silk shawl. "Yes, you are."

Against his will, Tenzin moaned. The demon's touch brought with it a pleasure that made his entire body vibrate, throb with need. The man's scent, a mixture of earth and musky sweat, passed into Tenzin's senses and made his *likpa* harder. The tide of pleasure engulfing him threatened to drown out his years of meditation.

"You will enjoy all the pleasures I will show you. The world is ours from which to feed." The demon slid his fingertips onto Tenzin's robe. "Men, women, no matter," he went on. "You will have them all. Pleasure will be your existence." The demon yanked at the coarse material of his monk's robe, and Tenzin an intense mixture of cool air and body heat on his bared chest. The demon slid a hand over the left side of Tenzin's chest.

Tenzin sucked in a breath and arched his back. His body seemed to have a will of its own, uncaring of his lifelong struggle with his desires. The demon seemed to sense his physical submission to the call of pleasure.

Suddenly, the demon's head jerked up. His hand froze where it lay, and he stared down at Tenzin. "This cannot be."

Tenzin felt his heart pound under the warmth of the demon's hand. "What cannot be?" The lust this stranger had stirred up in Tenzin still spiralled through his body.

"Your heart still beats."

"Should it not? You obviously did not kill me."

The demon growled. "I've sired you. You *cannot* still be alive."

Again, that arrogance. Tenzin sat up. Alive or not, he did not want to be under this creature's control. He had never even belonged to the mother and father who'd created his body. The remembrance caused new strength to surge through his limbs. "As long as my heart beats in my chest, only Lord Buddha is my master."

"You're *mine*." The demon curled his lips back as if to prove domination by showing his fangs.

Tenzin clenched his fists under his robes. His blood coursed hot through his body, and he found himself willing to fight this demon for his freedom.

The demon glared at him. The glow of bloodlust once again lit his eyes. "You're coming with me."

Tenzin sprang to his feet and returned the demon's hard stare. Raw physical power infused every muscle in his body. "I will not!" He felt his own eyeballs heat, saw the glow of them reflected on the demon's cheeks. The pressure of fangs extending from his gums filled him with a sense of power. Without thinking, he reached out and clutched the demon's shoulder.

The man-creature's eyes widened. A look of fear flashed through their depths. His mouth dropped open, and he trembled as if seeing the most frightening creature imaginable in front of him. He thrashed out of Tenzin's grasp, whirled around, and fled the cave.

Tenzin let out a deep breath. His fangs itched, and the heat receded from his eyes. All he heard was the whistle of the cold wind outside the cave.

For what felt like a long time, he stood and stared through the mouth of the cave, his fists clenched, ready to fight should the demon return. What had caused the creature to run away as he had? All Tenzin had done was touch him.

Tenzin lowered himself back onto his pallet and resumed the lotus posture. He tied his robes up around his body and made the *mudra* with his hands. He closed his eyes and called on his *mantra*. Instead of the holy word resounding in his mind, images barraged him, memories of the feel and scent of the demon's kisses, the icy heat of that tongue on Tenzin's nipples.

Tenzin let the images pass. He didn't fight them or hate them. The images shifted. He saw a woman, a beautiful woman with smooth golden skin and ripe breasts. Her dark nipples gleamed with promise and she laid back, thighs spread so that Tenzin could see the soft, inviting folds of her sex. He'd never laid eyes upon a naked woman in his life, but somehow he knew that his imaginings were true.

His cock hardened again. His mouth watered with the desire to smell and taste that hidden part, to bury his *likpa* deep inside it. The need was as raw, as powerful as it had been under the demon's erotic thrall.

The images never ceased. He squeezed his eyes shut and remained faithful to his *mantra* in spite of the burning needs of his body. He pulled a string of prayer beads from the depths of his robe and counted off a bead for each beat of the mantra. Perhaps if he meditated long enough, the craving would subside, as it had in the past.

He was wrong. In the several days that followed, the cravings worsened. The hunger returned and rumbled deep in his belly. With a will of its own, Tenzin's body rose from the pallet and drove him through the mouth of the cave, to the world beyond. He let himself be led, driven by the instincts he'd struggled so long to master, to a place where he could get blood.

Horrified at his ache to taste coppery, sweet blood, he knew his body would never rest until the hunger was satiated.

And his soul would not rest until he could find someone to help him tame his desires.

# Chapter One

*Sexual energy is the reason a human is born. Lack of sexual energy is the reason a human dies. Within this sexual energy is the secret not only of health but of immortality as well.*
–Madame Lin from *The White Tigress Manual*

*Shanghai, 1899*

*So this is what it had come to.* A game of cards to win herself a decent Green Dragon.

Lily could barely repress her disgust as she descended into the gambling parlour. She hated this place, hated the way men and women offered themselves willingly to be won for pleasure, and yet it was where the Chien Tung stick had sent her.

For years, she'd hoped for a Jade Dragon, a man who could actually become her steady partner on the White Tigress path. But most men could not bear a strong woman who took charge of her own body. It was a rare man indeed who could rise to the level of Jade Dragon. So, she would have to settle for a Green Dragon, a man to impart to her his *yang* essence. Of course, she could always go to Plum House, but she'd set that brothel up for her Tigresses to harvest *yang* from customers. As mistress, she did not mix with her students. Nor did she interfere with the male students who came to her school and partnered with the female students.

18

So it was the gaming parlour for her. She was weakening rapidly for a reason she couldn't explain. Her immortality had stabilised at age thirty, but that was nearly two centuries ago. In desperation, she'd finally given in and consulted the Chien Tung sticks. *Where may I find the man I seek?* she'd asked and shaken the fortune sticks, letting them spill on the ground in front of her altar. She reached down, chose the up-facing stick, and read it. She'd pulled in a shocked breath at the answer, but had heeded it anyway. *Very good fortune in the game,* the stick had said.

Lily kept her gaze forward as she reached the steps that would take her into the parlour. Her green silk *cheongsam* hugged her body like a second skin, making her descent of the steps a bit tricky. The high slits in the sides of her dress, perfect for showing off the pale smoothness of her legs, also gave her just enough movement to maintain her dignified pace and not fall flat on her face. The fact that her feet remained unbound also helped, even though her inability to have had that custom practiced on her as a little girl had cost her dearly.

A round of five-card stud was just being announced when she reached the doorway. A cloud of cigarette smoke wafted out into the dim corridor, the aroma of the cloud mixed with the scents of opium, rice wine, whisky, and blood in the various glasses on the edge of the gaming table. She squelched the urge to wrinkle her nose. As a Tigress, she did not partake of intoxicants. Being an immortal and not a vampire, she had no taste for blood, either.

Silence descended over the players and all eyes turned to her.

She returned their stares, keeping hers cool and level, rather than allowing her own curiosity to show. A Tigress maintained the upper hand at all times.

To the untrained, mortal eye, the place and its array of occupants in the smoky, Western-style parlour appeared like any other. Red damask wallpaper covering the walls, the brass gas lamp sconces casting shadows over the potted palms flanking the doorway and the faces of the players, men and women both Chinese and European. But after more than two centuries of life, she was schooled in every nuance of appearance that distinguished a werewolf from a vampire, from an immortal like herself, to a mortal human. Every manner of kith and kin was represented here, all beings—with the exception of a few mortals—with eternity on their side and not much else to fill it with but the pursuit of pleasure.

A white gentleman in a frock coat, his gold hair combed back, cheeks sporting thick sideburns, stood and bowed to her. He moved aside, surrendering his seat to her.

She nodded and walked to the out-held chair. Her eyes fell on the man's hand where it rested on the top of the chair, recognising immediately the crooked thumb that identified him as a werewolf. He assisted in pushing her chair to the edge of the gaming table and remained standing behind her.

The dealer resumed play, doling out cards to the participants of that round. Lily scanned the cards and then the players' faces. She could very often estimate a player's hand by the expression on his or her face.

This was more difficult in the underground parlours, as her opponents, also immortals, had had centuries to perfect their poker faces as well as their skills. One particular female, a vampire, strikingly beautiful, wore a slightly smug expression. Lily marked her as the one to beat.

Lily then noticed on the platform behind the table, where the prize of the current round of cards stood. She appraised the slim, elegantly muscular male, eyeing his sculpted form, nearly naked but for the white loincloth around his hips. Clear, blue eyes stared back at her from a chiselled face, his dark blond hair thick and full.

Lily felt the undeniable stirring in her loins. No doubt this man could bring her body much pleasure. Unlike most Chinese, she and her Tigress cubs were unconcerned about the ethnicity of their partners. They did not even refer to the white men as ghosts, the way their countrymen did. This man would be as welcome as a Chinese into their midst.

But for one thing.

He was a vampire. Though he gave no outward signs, she knew there was no heart beating under that muscular chest of golden downy hair. Aside from the fact that a vampire's *qi* could not nourish a human, those clear blue eyes would glow with bloodlust when she knelt between his thighs. That was fine for someone who desired such a partner, but Lily would rather be dragged to hell by a six-headed *yaojing* than couple with a vampire. Never again.

She averted her gaze so as to divert the desire fanning in her jade gate. Her breasts had begun to swell, nipples pushing against the tight *cheongsam*. She took as deep a breath as her dress would allow and waited patiently for a round that would bring a prize for whom she'd play.

The next round yielded a Chinese, stocky and robust, a labourer from what she could surmise. His golden muscles glowed, obviously oiled to show their perfection. Lily let her gaze rove over the man whose Manchurian queue of hair hung down the centre of his broad back in a thick braid. He turned, giving all players a clear view of his body, rounded, meaty thighs and sloping calves, carved abdomen and chest, arms sculpted strong from obvious physical labour. The bulge in his loincloth hinted at a well-endowed jade stalk. His face, too, was pleasant enough, his features firm and smooth, eyes narrow under arching brows. He was mortal, a regular human, and Lily felt a stirring of desire in her sex.

She looked closer, into the man's eyes. No good. In their brown depths, she saw the capacity for aggression, someone who did not succumb so easily to direction. Although he was a coolie accustomed to working for a boss, the glint in his eyes showed her he'd had enough of that submission, and she knew she couldn't risk subjecting herself to such a man. No matter how much pleasure she gave him, he would want to subjugate her and could grow violent at any moment.

She sighed inwardly and settled back. The dealer's gaze passed over hers, and she shook her head again. A servant came by with a tray, offering a choice of rice wine, whisky, or blood. Again, she gave a brief shake of her head and kept her eyes trained on the platform where the next male offering ascended the steps.

Her breath caught. She watched him, rapt, as he came to a standstill in front of the players.

She moistened her lips as her gaze travelled over his near-naked form. The soft light from the gas lamps glowed on his smooth, slightly oiled skin, the hue of toasted almonds, chest unmarred by any hair. In contrast to the stocky man before him, this man's build was slim, though his musculature was well developed. Lily's eyes spanned his chiselled torso, admiring the wide shoulders that tapered down to a slender waist. His stomach was board flat, the navel a small indentation. A thin strip of black, silky hair swirled down towards his groin.

Lily narrowed her eyes on the white loincloth, judging the man's most important endowment through the bunched-up cloth. The bulge of his dragon was clearly outlined, as was the apparently heavy sac of his *yang* pearls. A man of his build often possessed a deceptively small jade stalk and lacked in life force. Not this man.

To her shame, her mouth began to water. This man seemed to overflow with life force. Indeed, the energy that simmered off his muscular form conveyed to Lily his need to have the excess tapped off. With such abundant, ripe *qi*, he most certainly was *not* a vampire.

As was custom, the man turned his slow circle of display, giving the audience a clear view of his back. The gleaming expanse of muscles flexed with his movements, and again Lily felt her body's immediate response to him. He turned gracefully, his fluid motion an alluring contrast to his carved physique.

A narrow strip of loincloth ran down the crevice of his backside, exposing most of his hard buttocks. Her gaze travelled eagerly over the smooth globes of muscle and rested there. Although she had already examined the part of him that was relevant to her purpose, she couldn't help admiring him further. Every inch of him seemed beautifully formed.

As if to prove her thought, she finally tore her gaze away from his backside and let it move down to his legs. She'd been right. His thigh and calf muscles, covered with only a light sprinkling of hair, sloped with a sense of coiled power. Even his feet were beautifully shaped, and the callused heels did not appear rough and unsightly, but gave her the sense that he had travelled a long distance to be here.

He turned again and faced the players. Lily's gaze slid back up his body, over his well-endowed groin, carved stomach, and chest to his face. Her breath hitched again in her throat, and she used the last seconds before the game was called to study his face. He had the slightly rugged look of a man from the mountainous interior of China in the north. Was he Chinese? She wasn't certain. Realising she'd let her perusal of his body break her Tigress's concentration, she forced herself into her previous mind frame — that of a priestess examining a subject to deem his worthiness as a potential Jade Dragon.

He had a very pleasing face, lips full but not pouty, beautifully sculpted, the upper lip arched, his jaw clean-shaven. His face, oval-shaped but with high cheekbones, brought her gaze to his eyes, the very mirror to his character that would make her decision.

The dealer announced the next round of five-card stud. Only mere seconds left in which to decide. She looked into the man's eyes. Their gazes locked. His expression was even, yet the golden-brown disks of colour burned with passion. Passion, and a desire to —

The man next to Lily raised his hand, and the dealer put a down card at his place.

Lily held her breath, continuing to stare at the man on the platform. His gaze seemed locked on hers, as if he were silently drawing her to the game. She maintained her stare, waiting to see what he would do. In the next heartbeat, he lowered his gaze the tiniest bit and bowed his head. Respect without fear.

*Perfect.* She nodded to the dealer, who put a down card at her place.

Lily turned up the corner of the card. Ace of clubs. She let the corner down and watched the up cards of each player as they were dealt.

Her heartbeat rose as her hand was laid out before her. Ten... Jack... Queen... and King of clubs. *Gods!* Her hidden ace had become the ace in the hole she needed to win. With such a hand, she needed to keep her expression even.

Around her, players folded, one after the other. Except for one.

The vampiress Lily had observed earlier. Three nines were showing on the table before her. No doubt she had a nine in the hole. A nearly impossible hand to beat. The creature's ruby-red lips barely concealed a gleeful smile. Her beauty was marred only by the baleful glitter in her eyes. Behind her chair, another vampire stood, one large hand on her shoulder. Both wore beautiful silks and were groomed to perfection. There was something vaguely familiar about her, but Lily was certain she'd never seen her before. Not surprising. Kith and kin sometimes travelled great distances to participate in the floating underground game. Seeing the prize to be won from this round, Lily understood why. He was magnificent, perfect for her Tigress practice, if her judgement was as accurate as usual.

The Chinese she-vampire looked up at Lily, her eyes narrowing, a satisfied grin curving her reddened lips. Lily felt a distinct tightening in her chest.

This was it. Time to call her hand. Lily suppressed a grin. A ripple of murmurs erupted around the table. A face-off like this happened rarely and lent an air of added thrill to the game.

"Ha!" The vampiress turned over her down card, the nine Lily had suspected. Glee shone in her eyes. "Four of a kind."

Excitement skittered through the crowd.

Lily glanced at the man on the platform then back at her opponent. Now it was her turn to smile. "Not so fast, Madame." She picked up her down card, the ace that was — indeed, her ace in the hole — and set it with her four other cards.

Gasps and murmurs rippled through the onlookers.

The smile drained from the she-vampire's red lips, and her eyes narrowed to angry slits.

"Game goes to the royal straight flush," the dealer proclaimed.

Applause erupted, and Lily allowed herself a brief, modest smile. A Tigress was gracious at all times and never celebrated another's defeat.

Pushing back her chair, she rose and nodded to the man she'd won. He returned her gesture and let himself be led off the platform.

The werewolf who'd ceded his chair to her bowed politely and moved aside. Lily thanked him and went to the back waiting room where the players retrieved their winnings.

In the small waiting room, Lily perched on the edge of a chair, her hands folded around her reticule. He seemed to be taking too long to dress, but perhaps her anticipation made the moments seem longer. Her thoughts wandered to this man's identity. There was an air of refinement about him that made him unlike the majority of men who ascended that platform in their loincloths.

Who was he, and why had he offered himself as a prize in this game?

The men and women who did so each had their own purposes. Some hoped to find a wealthy patron to serve and thus avoid a life of hard labour. Others wished only for pleasure or for the blood-heating effect of risk. Others just wanted to be desired. But this man? She did not sense any of these purposes in him.

Could she trust that the fortune stick had spoken the truth?

Movement in the hallway pulled her from her introspection. In the next moment, her prize appeared in the doorway. His physique was now covered by coolie clothing, baggy pants tied with a drawstring and a mandarin-style vest of shabby linen which didn't hide the smooth curves of his biceps, nor the lean strength of his forearms

He bowed his head then raised his gaze briefly to hers. Lily swallowed, unexpectedly caught by the dark amber of his irises. A frisson of heat travelled trough her body, and she used the movement of rising from her chair to break the spell. It had been a very long time since a man had made her nervous this way, and she almost rethought her winning.

*Very good fortune,* the stick had said. Even so, she still needed to give him the same up-close evaluation she did with any man one of her Tigresses brought to her temple as a possible partner.

"Come here," she murmured.

He obeyed, and Lily couldn't help staring at the covered portions of his body, remembering their sleek perfection. The rough cotton was almost an affront against the golden skin of those strong legs. The waist rode low, and Lily glimpsed the taut skin of his hips.

He approached her and bowed his head again. When he raised it, he wore the same lowered gaze that had made her decide to play for him.

She was almost sorry for her request. As soon as he drew closer, his masculine aroma engulfed her. Musky yet strong and sweet, his scent curled inside her and heightened the erotic effect begun while watching him on the platform The pulsing in her sex increased, and she felt the fullness within her jade gate, the moist, swollen quality of sexual arousal that made her vividly aware of it with the smallest movement she made.

Male energy radiated off him. Surprisingly, the quality of that energy was not rough or aggressive as it was with so many males. In spite of the excess of *yang* she sensed in him, the quality of his *qi* was strangely soothing. She took a deep breath and continued her evaluation.

She took a tiny step back. "Look at me," she said softly.

He raised his face and looked at her. He was a full head taller and tilted his face down to meet her eyes. He wore an even expression, unchanged, though the amber colour within his eyes still burned with passion.

Ignoring her body's response, Lily forced herself to remain outwardly cool as she evaluated him. Since he wasn't a vampire, he was either human or a non-vampire immortal. The intensity of his male aroma led her to believe he was an immortal. Well, if he was as promising as he appeared to be, then his immortality was in her favour as well. Silently, she thanked the fortune of her hand in the game that had won him.

She perused him one last time before her final decision and, once again, was captured by the prospect of his loins, now hidden under the baggy pants.

Her mouth suddenly dry, Lily pulled her gaze from his groin, reining in her un-Tigress-like impulse to strip him then and there and take his thick dragon into her mouth. There would be plenty of time to savour his charms once she got him back to the temple, time to admire, feel, and taste.

She nodded. "You will return with me."

Silently he bowed his head, then stood aside to let her pass.

Lily clutched her reticule and focused on walking within her tight dress, vividly aware of the man close behind her. Her body and mind hummed with the anticipation of running her hands over his body, of feeling the smooth golden skin and hard muscles. Her mouth almost watered again at her anticipation of tasting his dragon, feeling that pulsing life against her tongue.

Tonight would not be soon enough to begin gathering his life force.

# Chapter Two

*The male retains. The female absorbs. Heaven [male] creates, Earth [female] is receptive. The male is active and so seeks stillness. The female is still and so seeks activity – each must acquire the essence of the other to be complete.*
~Madame Lin from *The White Tigress Manual*

*Could this beautiful woman truly be his teacher?* Tenzin stared at her back as he followed her through the quiet streets. Judging from the alluring silk dress that hugged her curves and the paint on her face emphasising her delicate features, it seemed impossible that she was the one who could teach him to control his desires.

Yet, it was more than possible. Since the vampire in the cave had sired him, Tenzin had spent the first hours of every single day hunched over his *sa ghazong*, the sand-filled board on which he made his astrological calculations. No matter where he was in his travels, he'd made the painstaking calculations that had finally brought him here, to Shanghai, where the Heavens had deemed it auspicious for him finally to balance his energies.

The route they walked was very familiar to him, a thoroughfare of public houses and restaurants lit up in spite of the late hour. He'd walked up and down this street in search of the precise spot of his calculations. That location had turned out to be the gaming parlour.

At the time, he'd stared in disbelief at the shabby façade of the structure, several disabused market stalls behind which was the hidden entrance. By late evening, he'd presented himself to the silk-caftaned Manchurian who'd answered his ring at the door. Centuries of suffering and desperation had overridden his disbelief and had readied him to be won in a game of chance, readied him to be owned by the one whom the *sa ghazong* had deemed would be his teacher.

A breeze cut the warm night and brought a whiff of the woman's scent to his nostrils. Heady and sweet, like opium and plums. He'd smelled it even while he stood on the platform surrounded by the odours of tobacco, alcohol, and blood. She was an immortal, no doubt, though not a vampire. Perhaps that boded well, for he felt as if he needed eternity to master the cravings that had tormented him for centuries.

In the light of the dim gas lamps that punctuated their way, he stared at the alluring swells of her hips and buttocks under the tight dress. They moved with an undulating rhythm, and her pale, smooth legs peeked out from the slits of her dress with each step. The sight roused his desire to caress her skin, to taste it, and to bury his face in the hidden apex of her thighs. She looked so much like the woman in the erotic visions he had when he'd first been made a vampire. Just looking at the ripeness of her cherry lips, it had taken all his self-control not to get hard in front of all those people.

Her pace was even, unhindered by her feet, which, he noticed, remained unbound. Since coming to China, he'd noticed so many women hobbled along on feet as tiny as those of a deer. He found himself desiring to see this woman's feet. His very hands itched to take a foot in his grasp and caress it, to trace the contours of each toe with his fingertips.

She stopped in her tracks and turned to him. The gas light glowed off her smooth skin and in her dark eyes. The expression in them conveyed that she'd sensed his silent perusal of her body. She turned fully to him.

"Walk beside me," she said. "You're not a slave, and slavery is not my purpose for having won you."

He bowed his head. "I'm sorry."

Her expression softened slightly. She turned and resumed walking, and he took his place beside her. After several more moments, she turned off the main street and onto an alleyway. Warm lights glowed from the doorways of the buildings on this street too, and the air rang with women's laughter, the familiar sounds of brothels.

Tenzin glanced to either side of him and saw women, many of them dressed like his hostess, standing in the doorways. Again, his mind reeled. He'd already frequented places like these in his travels, more than he wished to remember. This was what he'd wanted to avoid. Where was this woman leading him, and what could the *sa ghazong* possibly have meant by this?

He followed her around a corner. The street was more solitary here, lit only by gas lamps flanking a large carved doorway. She approached the door, retrieved a key from the small sack she carried, and turned open the giant lock.

She turned to him, her delicate face barely visible under the summer moon. Tenzin could see the outline of her full lips, smooth, narrow nose, high forehead, and thick eyelashes. Her hair, obviously thick and long, was pulled up into a bun at the nape of her neck, but the moonlight showed the gleaming curve of her throat.

"Do you speak Shanghainese?" the woman asked.

Inwardly he grimaced at his need to sink his incisors into that perfect skin and drink her blood. Had he been a soulless creature like his sire, that's what he would have done. He nodded, having taught himself the Chinese dialect in the weeks he searched for the spot of his calculations. "I do."

She let out a breath. "You must never tell anyone of this place or bring anyone here," she whispered. "Do you understand?"

He bowed his head, aware of the urgency underlying her hissed statement. "You have my word." When he raised his gaze to her, he caught her staring, her full lips slightly parted.

She looked intently at him a moment longer, as if to assess his sincerity. Her look softened once again, and she nodded. "My name is Lily."

He bowed his head again. "Yes, Lily." Saying her name sent a pleasant ripple through his loins. Had the *sa ghazong* not been so precise and reliable for centuries, he would have turned right then and put as much distance as he could between himself and this alluring woman.

He watched her hand come out, pale in the moonlight, her nails long, painted red, he knew, from seeing them holding her cards in the parlour. Several silver bracelets circled her slender wrist. "Follow me." The rings tinkled together softly as she pushed open the door and went through.

Averting his gaze from her lush bottom, he followed Lily into the front hall.

"Mistress Lily!" A young woman materialised in a doorway. She shuffled forward on bound feet in a rustle of loose clothing, a long-sleeved linen shirt and dark baggy pants, and bowed to Lily. Waist-length ebony hair, pulled back off her face, revealed smooth, delicate features. Her radiant beauty was similar to that of Lily's. Tenzin's first thought was he'd been led to a brothel.

"Fei Liu." Lily returned the gesture of respect and indicated Tenzin. "Please welcome our guest."

The young woman darted a glance at him and smiled shyly. Truthfully, her expression seemed far too innocent for a woman of the night. She bowed her head to him, then turned back to Lily. "Should I serve you tea?"

"Yes. We'll be in my chambers."

The girl bowed again and shuffled back out through the doorway through which she had come.

Lily looked up at him, her expression unreadable. "This way."

Tenzin followed her through a corridor and out into a courtyard. The new surroundings contrasted with the alleyway that hid this place. Several flowering trees flanked the corners of the stone floor, the scent of jasmine perfuming the still night air. A *koi* pond off to one side reflected the moonlight, the surface of the dark water dotted with lotus flowers. Soft lights shone through the latticed walls, emanating from the rooms that lined the courtyard, and a hushed energy, a strange mixture of stillness and sexual hunger, permeated the entire area, strengthening as they neared one of the entrances.

The pleasant surroundings could not hold Tenzin's attention for long. He found his gaze once more drawn to Lily's swaying figure. His breathing deepened as he watched her climb the stone steps in her form-fitting gown. He had to hurry to follow her through a red-painted doorway into one of the softly lit rooms. His attention riveted on Lily's form, he barely noticed the room. When he did, he found the surroundings a perfect reflection of his hostess. Comfortable chairs, low tables, and, farther in, a bed and a small seating area of cushioned chairs and a low table on one side. His hostess was, apparently, a woman of wealth.

Lily indicated one of the cushioned chairs. "Please, have a seat. I'll be back in a few moments." She disappeared into an adjoining room, separated from the one he sat in by a beaded curtain.

In the next moment, the woman called Fei Liu appeared. She carried a tray, hobbling towards him. Smiling warmly, she set down a teapot and two small cups, bowed to him and disappeared the way she'd come in.

Steam curled from the spout of the teapot. He watched the wisps of steam, wondering how he would refuse a cup of tea, when he detected the scent of honey infused with the herbal mixture. He breathed a small sigh of relief. Like the other vampires of his strain, honey was the one substance aside from blood he could digest.

The tinkling of beads grabbed his attention away from the tea. He turned and caught his breath.

Lily had changed her tight dress for a sheer robe of pink silk. As she drew closer, he could discern the outline of her breasts through the gauze material. He swallowed at the sight of the dark circles of her nipples. She'd pulled the pins from her hair, which now hung to her waist, the ebony fall shimmering in the soft lighting.

He bowed his head, surreptitiously curling one fist on his lap under the table.

"Is something the matter?"

He didn't look up, but knew she drew closer only because her intoxicating scent perfumed the still air immediately around him. His heart pumped, and his cock, which had already been half hard their entire walk to this house, now filled and pushed against his trousers. He clenched his jaw. "Yes." It was against the tenets of his religion to lie.

He sensed her pause. Several moments passed before she spoke again. "Do you wish to tell me what it is?"

He hitched another tight breath and pushed his hands between his knees, squeezing them together. "I am supposed to learn to control my desires." His throat dried suddenly, and he cleared it before continuing. "I don't see how I can do so this way. I'm sorry."

She didn't answer, and he refused to look up. He heard soft movement followed by the clink of porcelain and the tinkle of liquid being poured into a cup. More soft movement, her scent intensified, and a cup of steaming, fragrant tea was placed on the table close by. Then she moved away, and he heard her lower herself into a seat.

"What is your name?" she asked. To his relief, she did not bid him to look at her.

"Tenzin. Tenzin Gayatsu." He half expected her to reject him, not being Chinese, but she said nothing, and he heard her pour a second cup of tea. He refused the temptation to look up and see her full red lips as she sipped her tea, or the delicate muscles of her throat work as she swallowed.

"Tenzin." She spoke the name softly with a tone of interest. "You're Tibetan?"

He nodded.

"May I ask you a question?"

"Of course."

"Are you a monk?"

The gentle way she asked the question eased a bit of his tension. He exhaled. "I was a monk…once. I…did not fit in there." That was true enough after he'd been bitten. "However, I still wish to…overcome my carnal desires."

"Why?"

He almost looked at her but didn't, afraid to enflame his already straining *likpa* to the point of pain. "Because they are illusions and therefore obstacles to enlightenment."

He heard her take another sip of tea and sensed her considering his words. "You're correct, Tenzin. However, if you fight your desires in the attempt to overcome them, then you treat them as if they are ultimately real. Such a struggle can have no end and only produce more suffering."

He whipped his head up, heart pounding suddenly. It was an answer no one had given him in all these years. He'd never expected to hear such words, especially from a woman who appeared so earthly and sensuous, so given to pleasure, but something in him knew she was right. Already her answer was like a soothing balm to the ache in his soul that had driven him across the world.

Lily smiled, and her dark eyes shone from the gentle lantern light flickering in the room. The glow cast a blue shine on her hair, and he was overcome by the desire to lunge forward and kiss her lips.

"Tenzin, is that why you were on that platform tonight?"

How would she react to the truth? "Yes." He bowed his head once again. "I came here seeking a teacher. I was told my teacher would find me in that place."

When she didn't answer, he dared to look up.

Her violet eyes were wide, and her lips parted as if she would speak, but she remained silent for what felt like a long time.

Outside, he could hear crickets chirping as he waited for her to answer.

"Do you believe I am that teacher?" Her voice was soft, nearly a whisper.

He nodded. "Yes. I...wasn't certain until this moment. When you said what you did about desire."

Again she remained quiet. He sensed her doubt, her fear, some roiling of emotions inside her he didn't understand because he didn't know her. Sudden fear ripped through him, fear that she'd send him away.

He shot up from his chair and fell to his knees at her feet. "Lily, if you can teach me to overcome desire," he murmured, "I surrender myself to you, body and soul."

Lily stared at Tenzin Gayatsu. He didn't know her at all and seemed to know nothing of her Tigress religion. Yet here he knelt in front of her, bowing to her as she had once bowed to her teachers.

She swallowed hard, resisted the urge to reach out and touch his short-cropped hair. "I will be honest with you. I, too, seek enlightenment, and have for a very long time. I chose to play for you because I need someone who will let me...harvest his *yang* force. It's the path of my religion. When the forces of energy are balanced and at rest, the soul can reach higher planes of consciousness. Do you understand?"

He lifted his gaze to hers. His dark eyes simmered with that same intensity she'd seen when he'd stood on the platform in his loincloth. Up close, the effect of his eyes was startling, intoxicating. He nodded and bowed his head again. "I'm not certain, Lily." His voice sounded strained, hoarse.

Softly she cleared her throat. "There are certain...exercises...you and I would perform together that are meant to balance our life force, our *qi*. A woman cannot do them alone, nor can a man. Both partners are needed. *Yin* and *yang* together." Without thinking, she put her index finger under his chin and tilted his face up to hers. The rasp of his clean-shaven skin was pleasant against the pad of her fingertip. To her surprise, a single tear rolled from his eye and slid down the smooth plane of his cheek. The droplet reached the edge of his jaw and fell onto her hand.

"Tenzin, have you ever been with a woman?" Certainly his response would affect how she proceeded. A completely inexperienced man would need much more time and training before he could be a steady partner in the Tigress-Dragon exercises.

He nodded then cast his gaze downward. "For a period of time, I indulged in pleasures of the flesh. It's been several years since. I've worked so hard to abstain, yet I have not been able to find the middle ground."

Lily smiled in a way meant to ease his discomfort. There would be time later to ask him the nature of his experiences. "You can make desire your ally, Tenzin," she said softly. She felt some of her apprehension drain as it always did when she spoke about the path of the White Tigress.

Remembering her role as instructor and spiritual aspirant balanced her once again. "Use your desire to overcome it. You neither indulge desire wildly nor deny it. Use it properly and like a splinter you can use it to remove another splinter." She stared into his eyes a moment longer, careful to glance away when the intensity of his gaze seemed as if it would trap her in its depths. "I would never force you to stay here and perform these exercises with me, Tenzin. Only a willing partner can help another. Are you willing to help me as I'm willing to help you?"

"Yes, I am," he said. "Please, teach me." Tenzin stared up at her. More tears slipped from his eyes and rolled freely down his cheeks.

She resisted the urge to brush his tears away with her thumb. Her heart quickened and a ripple of energy moved through her sex. For several moments, she watched his face, searched for some trace of dissemblance in it. She desperately needed to know that his willingness was not an act. Unfortunately, she had heard similar professions in the past. Some men *were* seeking something higher, but when it came down to the commitment of heart and soul, they ran, unwilling to make a woman their equal partner.

Tenzin didn't seem insincere, but she couldn't take any chances. She would begin by draining off his excess *yang* and proceed from there. In his present condition, he was desperate and such a state did not indicate true commitment. There was just as good a chance he would respond like many of the other men she'd worked with in the past who, once they had attained a certain level of comfort, could no longer stand having a woman in the position of teacher.

Finally she nodded. Her body heated with nervous energy; her hands trembled slightly. She rose from her chair. "Come then," she said. "We'll begin now."

# Chapter Three

*The* yin *absorbs the* yang, *the* yang *absorbs the* yin — *this secret is so simple it goes unnoticed and undetected.*
~Madame Lin from *The White Tigress Manual*

Lily led Tenzin to her bath chamber where Fei Liu had filled the tub with steaming, scented water. Fei Liu stood, her head bowed, an empty bucket hanging from her hands. From the corner of her eye, Lily saw her favourite Tigress cub steal a glance at Tenzin.

A sliver of guilt stabbed Lily that she was keeping Tenzin to herself. Normally, she gave Fei Liu a chance to practice the exercises with a man of whom she had approved. Lily told herself that Tenzin was too green, too in need of preparation, and must remain with the experienced teacher.

"Do you need anything else, Mistress Lily?" Fei Liu's voice was soft and conveyed her admiration of the man before her.

"No, thank you, Fei Liu." Lily made certain her tone dismissed the woman, gently but firmly.

Fei Liu nodded and shuffled from the room on her bound feet.

Alone with Tenzin, Lily was eager to see his body naked. Her heartbeat sped up slightly, and she took a deep breath before turning her attention to him. When she did, the Tibetan stood, hands at his sides, his gaze humble yet still simmering.

She appraised him a moment longer. So far, the fortune sticks had spoken the truth. Tenzin's eyes radiated compassion and devotion while his body emitted a sense of coiled strength and power, even through the worn, baggy clothing.

Before having him undress, she scanned every inch of his sleek, muscular body, lingering on the sheen of his dark golden skin, the carved strength of his arm muscles, his high, dignified cheekbones, as well as the sensuous pout of his lips surrounded by the darkness of clean shaven cheeks and jaw. Lily's body tingled, and already she felt her *yin* dew rise, as it had in the gambling parlour. Her female energy rendered her body softer and more pliant in accord with his male hardness. "Undress, please," she said, affecting the silky tone customary for a Tigress in the process of seduction.

Tenzin's hands went to the frog closures of his vest. Thick, strong fingers worked open the wooden toggles until the rumpled fabric fell open, revealing his smoothly muscled chest. His pectorals were wide and round, topped with dark, cocoa brown nipples.

Lily watched him slide the vest off, down his strong arms, gazing at him with the appreciation intended to bolster his confidence. In this instance, her enjoyment was entirely sincere, and when his cheeks coloured slightly, she averted her eyes enough to allow him to collect himself.

Unlike most other men she'd practiced with, Tenzin shed his clothes slowly, with a sense of modesty that made him seem vulnerable. With each small movement, the cords of muscle in his forearms flexed, as did the carved muscles of his abdomen. Her heartbeat rising, Lily stepped forward and took his vest from him. She folded it and set it on a nearby chair before turning to watch him remove his pants.

With his eyes downcast, he pulled the drawstring of his pants and held the waist so they wouldn't drop at his feet. His thigh muscles clenched as he lifted each foot and carefully stepped out of his pant legs. Again she reached out and retrieved his pants, resisting the urge to stare blatantly at his round, hard buttocks.

He surrendered his clothing, an uncertain look moved across his eyes. Lily allowed her fingers to brush against his, enjoying the surge of *yang* force she sensed in him. The musky scent of his skin mingled in the air heated from bath water and herbs. Her insides jumped, and she took a deep breath as she set the remainder of his clothing on the chair.

She turned and nearly gasped. *Yin* surged in her body, and she felt her feminine instinct to melt against Tenzin's hard physique. It wasn't time yet for that. She turned halfway from him and gestured towards the tub. "I hope the water is to your liking," she said in a silky voice.

"It looks very nice," she heard him say. "I am grateful for the luxury."

His gratitude sounded genuine, and this only fuelled her natural instinct to join with him. Lily surreptitiously squeezed her hands into fists and dug her nails into her palms, anything to stem her *yin* tide and distract herself from staring at his naked physique.

The lower part of the man was as beautifully formed as the top. His trim waist tapered into narrow hips, which drew her gaze to what was in the centre. His dragon was thick and full, just as the contours of it through the loincloth had hinted. The reddish-gold shaft stood in a partial erection, and the tapered head, plump and very suckable, had already seeped a glistening dragon's tear at the tiny opening. The *yang* droplet made her very mouth water to lick it off.

Tenzin's dragon twitched as if aware of her gaze on it. His body was nearly hairless with the exception of a small ebony thatch around the base of his dragon. That sight roused the most intense need within her to taste him, to feel what looked like velvety skin over the hardness of male muscle.

Lily allowed herself a brief perusal of the full sac of his *yang* pearls below his dragon, then slid her gaze down his thick, sloping thighs and calves.

She cleared her throat. "Go on. Get in."

He nodded. "Thank you." His eyes reflected uncertainty, but he turned, obedient, and stepped into the tub, giving Lily a perfect view of his bottom.

She moistened her lips with the tip of her tongue. Tightening her fists, she wondered at the effect he was having on her. The only explanation certainly was his overabundance of *yang*, causing the imbalance happening within her own body.

Tenzin held the sides of the tub, strong fingers gripping as he lowered his powerful build into the water. Judging by the delicious scent that emanated from him and his obviously clean appearance, he didn't need a bath, but the ritual of washing a man, relaxing him, ministering to him as she was about to, was what a Tigress did with her partner. The more at ease he was and comfortable, the more freely his *yang* would flow.

She knelt by the tub. Tenzin's male scent, diffused into the air by the steamy water, surrounded her. She cleared her throat with as delicate a sound as she could, in spite of the sudden tightness.

Picking up a washcloth, she dipped it into the hot water and smoothed it across his back. The water streamed down his muscles. She wet the cloth again and ran it over his neck.

A tiny sigh escaped the Tibetan's throat. He took a deep breath, and his shoulders sagged ever so slightly. His eyelids fluttered, and his fingertips relaxed their grip on the sides of the tub.

She frowned. Could he be nervous? She never thought of men as nervous, especially with women, the power-wielding creatures the other sex were... She couldn't imagine it. Men had the power to determine whether a girl underwent the painful, harrowing process of having her feet bound, or of being enslaved for life to a man who could beat her with impunity. And yet, she was forced to admit, she'd never met a man who'd bowed down before her as this one had. She could only imagine he would be nervous about being with a woman again after his long abstinence.

Lest he see her musing, she worked her lips into a smile and continued to wash him. With a hand on his shoulder, she bid him to lean back in the tub. The hard muscle quivered under her fingertips, but he yielded under her touch, letting her guide him to recline in the tub.

A slice of heat went through her middle, and Lily avoided his eyes until she could collect herself. When she did look at him, his gaze locked with hers. He regarded her through half-closed lids. His amber irises simmered with the strangest blend of wonder and need. Droplets of water beaded off his skin, and a sheen of moisture from the steam made his skin glow. He parted his full soft lips as if he were about to speak but remained silent, and she could hear the steady pulse of his slightly ragged breaths.

Swallowing past the dryness in her throat, she lifted her hand from his shoulder. "Give me your hand," she said softly.

He slid up a bit in the tub, giving Lily a glance of his dragon, harder than it had been before. The plump lobes of the head were visible even through the depths of the water. With that wondrous gaze still on hers, he lifted his hand, surrendered to her hold.

Lily took his hand between hers, smoothed her fingertips gently over the callused skin of his palm, and then looked at it. Tenzin's fingers were wide and strong, the hands of a man who worked hard, yet whose nails were perfectly clean and trimmed. A strange blend of contradictions, this man was. He appeared poor, but his worn clothing was clean and smelled of the spicy musk that he carried on his skin. Perhaps he'd simply cleaned himself up before presenting himself as a prize in the card game. That seemed the most logical answer.

She began to massage the palm of his hand, pressing gentle circles into the soft flesh below his thumb. Again, he sighed, the soft whoosh of breath almost a moan. His fingers curled slightly, and his hand grew more slack between hers. Lily couldn't help the flush of pleasure she felt in seeing that he seemed to enjoy her ministrations so much.

"May I ask you something, Lily?"

She glanced at him, careful not to let her gaze get captured in his again. His penetrating look made her feel strangely beautiful, yet completely, abashedly, naked all at once. The former feeling, of course, was not something in which a Tigress should indulge.

"Of course. You may ask whatever you wish." She kept her gaze on his hand while she kneaded and rubbed the callused mounds of flesh at the base of each finger. Truthfully, she was relieved for conversation that would take her concern away from the aroused state she entered from touching him.

"Are these *yin* and *yang* exercises part of a religion you practice?"

"What makes you ask?" She looked at him and immediately realised her mistake. Those eyes, mysterious, childlike and sensual all at once, trapped her.

"Just a feeling."

She continued her gentle massage of his hand, worked her touch up the length of each wide, strong finger. "Yes. I practice the Path of the White Tigress. It's the use of life force in the Taoist tradition to achieve enlightenment."

"Through eroticism."

She found his seemingly genuine interest encouraging. His questioning, too, was a rare trait. Most men simply wanted her to get onto her knees and suck their *jiaos* as soon as possible. "That is correct." She, herself, hadn't reached the higher levels of enlightenment since the early years of her practice, but she didn't tell him this. When she'd begun the practices as a Tigress cub under her teacher, Tigress Mai, Lily had reached the Place of One Hundred Returnings.

However, at some point, her practice had waned, probably because she had not been able to find a decent steady partner, concentrating instead on instructing the women who came to her. For them, the Temple of the White Tigress was not only a place to seek enlightenment, but also a safe haven for women, former prostitutes and abused wives, who needed shelter. As far as Lily was concerned, spiritual advancement was a gift if it happened. The women's safety and happiness were her primary concerns.

"I understand." His voice was unnervingly gentle, like a soft caress. "That explains your demand for my secrecy."

Now she stared at him straight on. When it came to her Tigress cubs, women for whom Lily struggled and toiled to keep off the streets and give purpose to their lives, she felt no fear or shame. "Women who do what we do are unwelcome in society, that is, except for the pleasure we give men's bodies." She heard the bitterness in her tone and paused. When she spoke again, she softened her words. "We must keep under to endure, as Lao Tzu said. Our lives depend on discretion."

"I give you my word that I'll be careful." His mysterious eyes looked directly into hers, and she had the sense he could see deep into her heart, past the seductive Tigress she'd made of herself, to the young woman who had been a vampire's slave for food and pleasure.

Heart pounding, she released his hand and went around the tub to massage his other hand, grateful for the distraction. "May I ask you a question, Tenzin?"

He bowed his head, then looked at her with that unfathomable gaze of his. The look that made her *yin* surge each time. "Anything, Lily."

Now that he'd shown her some degree of integrity, she felt she could proceed. "If we are to work together, I must know more about you. Can you please tell me something about your experiences?"

To her surprise, his cheeks coloured slightly. He was silent for a moment as she gently rubbed the calluses on his palms, pressing down with careful pressure into his skin.

"For a long time, as a monk, I was completely chaste," he said softly. "When I left the monastery, I wandered through Tibet, still abstinent. It wasn't until I reached northern China and went to a city that I indulged. There was a place called the House of the Jade Flower." He looked down. "I spent all my nights there for a long time. The women were kind and beautiful and giving." Finally he raised his gaze to hers again. Pain clouded the rich amber of his eyes. "It got so I couldn't bear the guilt, Lily. It was like I had a war raging inside me all the time. I forced myself to leave that place behind and wander again. Since then, I've tried everything to overcome my lusts, severe austerity, mortification of the flesh, sensory deprivation, endless chanting, and prayer, everything."

Tenzin glanced away again. "For a brief time, I went to India and there practiced the various religious paths. Nothing worked. I've consulted the Heavens every single day since I left the monastery, and only until this very night has it finally told me that the forces in the world and in my spirit were propitious enough to bring me to my true teacher."

Lily heard the desperation in his voice, felt it churn and swirl with the *yang* that overflowed in his body and spirit. Indeed the calluses of his hands and feet proved the miles he'd journeyed and amount he'd worked. The supplication and grief in his voice sounded real and was a sound she'd heard once before in Tigress Mai, who'd struggled and suffered to find the Taoist path she'd walked and imparted to Lily.

"I pray you believe me, Lily."

His voice pulled her gaze to his, and for the first time, she realised he was not ignorant of her responses to him. The plea in his sound sent a spike of guilt through her. Perhaps she was being too harsh in her reserve. She was falling into her own fears of being a victim again. But she wasn't a victim. After all, Tenzin wasn't a vampire. He was most likely an immortal, and as an immortal, if he tried to hurt her in some way, she had most of her physical strength to fight him, as well as years of Shaolin training. She could approach Tenzin as an equal, without fear. If they were to be partners, she would have to do so.

"I believe you," she said softly. "You seek a way out of suffering, as all beings do. I would not deny you any help that I could give."

As soon as she'd spoken, some of the grief drained from his face, and he bowed his head. Lily could hear the gratitude in his reverent silence.

Lily set his hand down gently and went to the end of the tub. She knelt down again and proceeded to rub Tenzin's feet. She massaged the soles, pressed her thumbs deeply into the callused skin. Again, the cleanliness of even his feet amazed her.

Tenzin groaned softly. "That feels so wonderful."

Again, Lily experienced the familiar sense of pleasure when she had a man exactly where she wanted him. With a minimum of words, the Tibetan exuded appreciation. She pulled herself in, careful to retain her distance. It wouldn't do to let go too soon. She had mastered the practiced way of giving passion with detachment that was the mark of the White Tigress.

The water in the tub sloshed gently. Lily felt Tenzin's body slide down a bit in the bath. He lay back, eyes closed, a tiny smile on his lips. His breathing had slowed, and she could see he was totally relaxed, so much so that his dragon now lay partially flaccid against one muscular thigh. His broad chest rose and fell steadily. Stillness hummed in the air.

Her hands tingled around Tenzin's foot. The energy cascaded gently into her wrists, flowed up her arms, a free flow of the Tibetan's *yang* energy, released by the massage.

The energy travelled into her breasts, down through her abdomen, into her sex, which tingled wildly. Her own body grew languid, yet her mind retained clarity and calm.

Amazing! *Yin* and *yang* had melded already and they hadn't even begun the exercises. She exhaled silently, preparing for the next stage. Her body and mind quivered with anticipation. Maybe this man *could* actually help her restore her strength? Or even better, enable her to reach the Place of One Hundred Returnings again?

Slowly, she straightened from her kneeling position, dried her hands on a small towel and reached for a larger towel, which she unfolded. When she looked at Tenzin, his eyes were closed. She touched his shoulder softly and showed him the towel.

His eyelids flickered, and he looked at her with a more serene gaze. Apparently, he too, had been calmed by the blend of their energies.

At her slight nod, he rose, the water splashing softly against the sides of the tub, his movements smooth and placid, his limbs relaxed, like a man rising from deep meditation.

Lily could not avert her eyes from his naked body, golden skin gleaming with droplets of water. His dragon, at rest now, hung partially sheathed, between his legs. Her fingers itched to surround it and bring it to life. It swung forward with the movement of his body as he climbed out of the claw-footed tub and stepped into the towel she held for him.

For a few seconds, she stood still, mere inches from him, separated only by the towel. His nearness to her skin once again stirred her *yin*. In spite of the calming they'd both experienced, the excess was still there in her as well as in Tenzin and needed to be drained off.

Before she grew too restless, she let the towel loosen and stepped around him.

Slowly, she brought the towel up to his back and began to rub it across his shoulders, patting it gently over the wide planes of his back muscles. The velvety sheen of his skin replaced the watery glow as she dried him. She worked her way down his spine to his narrow waist, then over his firm buttocks. She couldn't help touching their smoothness with her bare hands and resisted the temptation to peek around to see what her ministrations were doing to the front side of him.

There would be time enough...

She proceeded to dry the narrow space between his legs, stopping short of coming in contact with his *yang* sac, just visible to her. As if reading her thoughts, he shifted his legs, widened them an inch so she could have better access. But she declined the invitation, telling him with her gestures that it was she in control of this session.

She took her time rubbing down the length of his strong legs, the thighs and calves powerfully rounded, until she'd reached his ankles. She swiped over the tops of his feet and turned her attention to his front.

His dragon had hardened again. The thick member stretched its head from its sheath and stood in a jutting curve from his body. His breath rasped in her ears, and she could smell the heaviness of his male musk. Her *yin* responded, made her sex quiver and soften with slippery dew. Even the heavy sac beneath, plump and full of life force, made her salivate, long to trace the contours of each pearl with her fingertips, and then the tip of her tongue.

She patted the towel gently on his lower abdomen then brushed it around the base of his dragon. Reluctantly, she gave the delicious-looking member a last pat, promising herself that soon she would be revisiting it, this time with her mouth. She proceeded and wiped dry the hard edges of his pelvis, running her fingers through the wispy thatch of his pubic hair, and upward over his flat belly.

The soft towel readily absorbed the droplets of water off Tenzin's skin, just the way Lily intended to absorb his *yang* into herself. She ran the towel over his strong chest and longed to feel the hard bulges fill her palms. Even the dark brown shade of his nipples was perfectly matched to his skin and invited her to taste them. Keeping her attention firmly on the task at hand, she finished drying Tenzin's arms, letting the towel slide over the etched contours that separated his shoulder muscles from triceps and biceps. She bid him to raise each arm so she could swipe the towel underneath and dry the small thatches of dark hair in the musky recesses.

Her stomach fluttered suddenly as if a jarful of butterflies had been released inside her. Nervous! She paused at the unusual reaction, not recalling such a sensation since her first days as a Tigress. Back then the mere gaze of a man as handsome as Tenzin had made her perspire and shake. So many times she'd actually fumbled with a man's dragon as she knelt before him, only to feel the heat of embarrassment burn her cheeks. However, years of assiduous practice with men had long-since dissolved this childish response.

Why? Was it because of the strange, almost perfect balance of *yin* and *yang* she had just experienced in the tub? He was a man, a Green Dragon, a vessel from which she could sip his *yang* force, an aid to her in her quest for enlightenment, the only possible relief from the endless suffering and loneliness of the world. She reminded herself that once she'd achieved that end, she wouldn't need him anymore.

No doubt, he wouldn't need her either. Not that he ever had, or would. Men never did.

Her heart beat hard so loudly she could hear her own blood crash in her ears. Her mouth went dry, anticipating the feel and taste of his dragon. Turning slightly, she gestured to him. "This way."

# Chapter Four

*When the Dragon plays near the Tigress's mouth, the Tigress seizes
the fallen jade.*
~Madame Lin from *The White Tigress Manual*

Tenzin's heart pounded. Between Lily's body
showing through the sheer material of her robe, the
sensual bath, and the way she'd dried him, his *likpa*
felt as if it would explode. Having emerged from an
extended, failed period of sensual deprivation, he
hadn't known a woman's touch in the longest time
and feared he would spill himself too soon. Lily's
massage of his hands and feet, the small touch on his
shoulder, and her beauty all had made him wild with
desire for her.

If he hadn't caught several glimpses of the
vulnerable girl underneath the seductive Tigress, he
would have felt completely inadequate. Lily was
beautiful. He couldn't help staring at the way her
waist-length ebony hair swayed, how the tips brushed
the tops of her buttocks. Part of a tattoo covered one
creamy swell and wrapped around her waist to her
front. She walked with a balanced sway rather than
the shuffle of a woman with bound feet. Personally he
found her gait as seductive as the rest of her and could
imagine that any man might worry about his ability to
please a woman so magnificent and so obviously
practiced at seduction.

He followed her back into her bedchamber. The warm incense-scented air wafted around his bare skin. By the bed, she halted him with a small touch on his arm and turned her gaze up to his. Once again he saw her falter inwardly. He'd practiced observing people for far too long to miss the tiny flicker in her eyes that communicated a touch of nervousness or doubt. She'd done this several times in the course of the night, and each time it happened, he felt a bit less awkward, remembering her humanity. Underneath the lacquer and silk, underneath whatever method of erotic practices she followed, she was a woman, a being with fears and sufferings of her own.

She blinked and he noticed the contrast of thick ebony lashes against the creamy silk of her skin. "Are you ready to continue, Tenzin?"

The question alone sent a shiver of lust through him. Wordlessly, he nodded, unable to speak through the thickness in his throat.

"Well then, we shall." A tiny smile curved the red fullness of her lips. Slowly, she brought her hands to her robe and slipped it back. The pink silk whispered down her arms and fell to the floor.

Hot blood shot through his *likpa*. He looked down, face burning. Sweat erupted on his brow.

"Remember what I said earlier about desire." Lily's soft voice caressed him, eased a bit of his discomfort away. "Desire is a tool, an ally, when used correctly. I will help you use it correctly, Tenzin. Just look at me."

Slowly, carefully, he lifted his gaze to Lily's. Her perfect almond-shaped eyes, dark and sultry, regarded him with a potent blend of kindness and desire. Her smile deepened, this time, reaching her eyes. "Look at all of me, Tenzin. Every single inch."

His heartbeat increased. The flowery musk of her scent invaded his senses. In spite of the throbbing need in his lower regions, it wasn't so easy to give in to his desire, not after so many years of fighting with it.

"As your teacher, I give you absolute permission to stare at me."

*Must...obey.* He let his gaze move lower, to the delicate curve of her pale throat.

"Don't be afraid to look at my breasts, Tenzin." She paused and smoothed her hands over them in a way that drew his gaze. "Do they make you want to touch them?"

Tenzin looked at the ripe swells. He swallowed hard as he studied their shape, fuller on the bottom in a way that made them point upward. Her large nipples were dark, reddish brown, almost the colour of plum wine, and the skin of her breasts was temptingly pale and smooth. They rose and fell with her gentle breathing. He nodded again, his mouth watering to taste those dark, inviting tips.

She slid one hand, fingers splayed, down her flat stomach. Her red nails contrasted seductively with her pale skin then blended with the front part of the tattoo he'd glimpsed. "Look lower, Tenzin."

His eyes were now captured on the trail her hand made. Her fingertips grazed the contours of a colourful leaping tiger inked on her skin. He'd glimpsed before the creature's powerful long tail curl over the swell of one buttock, but now had a clear view of the rest of the tiger's body as it leapt upward, front claws extended towards one side of her ribcage, the creature's belly positioned over the front of her sex.

"What do you feel, Tenzin, when you look at me?"

He swallowed hard, his mouth and throat terribly dry. She turned and retrieved his tea cup from earlier. Someone had emptied it and replaced the cold tea with fresh, steaming liquid. The scent of honey stimulated some moisture in his mouth.

"Drink this before you answer," she said and held the cup to his lips.

He put a hand over hers and tilted the cup, letting the warm, sweet drink pool on his tongue. He swallowed greedily until the small cup was empty.

She smiled as she lowered the cup and set it aside. The tiger on her belly moved and stretched. "Is it easier to speak now?"

Tenzin swallowed. "Yes." In spite of the lubrication, his voice came out in a tight whisper. He stared at Lily's lower body, at the perfect flare of her hips and over her shaved pubic mound. In the haze of his mind, he could just remember her question. "I feel…"

"Yes? It's all right. No matter what you say."

His eyelids shuttered briefly and he glanced up into her eyes. Again, he was captured by the seductive yet compassionate shine in them.

"I…want you…Lily…" his body thundered, his cock throbbed, and words came with great difficulty, "…so much."

Lily's smile deepened, and he sensed that his words pleased her more deeply than what showed in her face. "Very soon now." She reached out, and her gentle touch on his shoulders urged him back onto the bed.

He felt his aroused body sink into a wealth of silk pillows. It had been so long since he'd lain in such a bed with a woman, and Lily's bed seemed to invite two lovers to entwine themselves in its softness.

Lily knelt in front of him. The top of her head just reached a level with his lips and the fragrance of her hair and skin, like jasmine flowers mixed with female musk, intoxicated him. He wanted to reach out and pull her against him and take her mouth in a deep kiss. His lips ached to taste hers, to explore the soft, warm recesses of her mouth with his tongue.

But he held back, not only because he was her student now, but because he sensed her *need* for control. In spite of their respective roles, something about Lily called on his deepest powers of restraint. Of respect.

"I want you, too, Tenzin," Lily said softly. She ran her hands down his arms and rested her touch on his forearms. In spite of the vast erotic experiences he'd had in the past centuries, heat bloomed in his cheeks. The feeling was so strange, as if this were his first time with a woman. He didn't understand the effect Lily had on him and could only attribute it to the fact that she was, indeed, his first woman in a long time and that she was knowledgeable about men. Perhaps she'd compare him to others and find him lacking.

He pulled his mind away from such thoughts. He was here to give her his *yang* force, an act which would help them both. Lily was a Tigress, a religious practitioner, someone who certainly did not need a man beyond the life force that flowed from his body.

Lily tilted her heart-shaped face upward. Her violet eyes studied him, her full soft lips slightly parted. She reached up and placed her hands, palm down onto his chest. Her light touch sent a ripple of heat straight to his now aching groin. His breath hitched, and he watched her, surrendered to the tingling warmth where her skin touched his.

"Just allow yourself to enjoy my touch." She slid her hands up, grazing his nipples.

Tenzin sucked in a breath. He moaned softly as his nipples pebbled under her soft caress.

"That's it," she crooned. "Just relax."

Tenzin watched her, gaze trapped by her caress. He sensed so many thoughts and feelings swirl inside her, things she wouldn't say out loud but which carried through her touch on his skin.

Her fingers remained splayed on his shoulders, her eyes narrowed slightly, the lids sensually heavy.

He resisted another impulse to reach out and pull her into his arms. How much more would she make him endure? His cock was already harder than a diamond, the skin seeming to be stretched to its limit, the veins ready to pop. At this point, she could do anything she wished to him, and he would obey.

He willed himself to remain quiet, his training in meditation standing him in good stead. His heavy breathing was the only indication of how close he was to losing all control.

She slid her hands on his shoulders and leant into him. The warmth of her body invaded the narrow space between them. She closed the distance, let her breasts brush his chest, and pressed her lips softly to his lips. The kiss was quick, like a single breath. She brushed her bottom lip across his with a mere whisper of touch.

His eyelids shuttered, and his lips parted, wanting to receive more. That little taste of her mouth, and the tiny swipe of her nipples against his skin, made his head swirl and stole all rational thought from his mind. His heart thumped in his chest, a steady rapid beat, while his cock stood almost straight up.

Involuntarily, he jutted his hips forward, as if to reach the moist warmth of her sex.

But she seemed to draw back from him. She stared up at him, her eyes wide as if startled. What had frightened her? In the next second, the sensual Tigress demeanour slid back into place, and he wondered if he'd imagined the split-second of fear.

She slid her hands from his shoulders back down to his chest. The movement, though sensual, was obviously practiced. She trailed her fingertips down the furrow that divided his two chest muscles. Her touch left a trail of tingling heat, teased him more, and made his cock surge to the point of pain.

A tiny smile curved her lips, and her eyelids hooded her eyes as she trailed her feather light touch back over his nipples. With the pads of her index fingers, she swirled tiny circles over the sensitive disks, which tightened again. Icy heat sparkled through his chest, and Tenzin closed his eyes and tilted his head back, barely able to support his weight under the pleasurable assault.

Energy swirled in his chest, seemingly pulled by her touch. Wherever Lily's fingertips went, the tingling heat followed.

Tenzin forced himself to open his eyes. He wanted to watch Lily touch him, wanted to keep his gaze on her beautiful face, her pouting lips, painted the red of cherries, as well as the darker flush of pink in her smooth cheeks. Her own nipples had tightened, he noticed, eyeing the dark peaks. He almost reached out and cupped her breasts, desperate to feel the soft swells against his hands. He pulled in a shuddering breath. When would she let him touch her?

Lily's touch slid to his back, slender arms encircling him. The movement brought her closer, so close that her breath pulsed warmly onto his skin. Leaning in, she pressed her lips to the centre of his chest.

He released a shuddering sigh. The soft pressure of Lily's mouth on his skin was exquisite. She parted her lips, brushed them back and forth. Each tiny slide of her full mouth made his skin tingle, made his shaft tighten more and more.

The tip of her tongue darted out and slid up the centre furrow of muscle with moist warmth. He sucked in his breath, and his hands, on reflex, slid into her ebony hair. His chest rose and fell heavily under her seeking tongue, which she trailed teasingly to one side, tracing the outlines of his muscles and feathering a trail across to one nipple. The moist heat of her mouth closed over the sensitive, flat round.

*Ohhh.* His fingers tightened in her sleek hair. She flickered the tip of her tongue several times over the hard tip, then tugged it between her lips and tongue, gentle, sensual pulls that sent shoots of heat straight into his groin.

"Lily." Her name slipped from him before he could stop himself. He stiffened, wondering whether she would pull away.

Instead, she pressed her hands into his back, bringing him closer. She lifted her mouth an inch away from his skin and blew over his moistened nipple. The soft, cool wind of her breath caressed the aroused peak. Tenzin curled his fingers deeper into her hair.

He tilted his head back, lost in the sensations—the wet heat of her mouth on his skin, the sleekness of her hair against his fingertips, the gentle press of her hands on his back, expertly teasing his body to the heated arousal only her soft, wet petals could relieve.

Lily pressed her lips into his skin again, kissing a soft trail over to the other side of his chest. She closed her lips over his other nipple and tugged the tight bud against her tongue. More sparks of heat darted through his body, travelled in an invisible trail to his groin. He groaned softly, whispered her name again.

This time she did lift her head, causing his hands to slip from her hair. Her eyelids were heavy, her full lips parted, gleaming from her kisses to his chest. The scent of her arousal filled the air, making him feel crazed with lust and wishing she would entwine her body with his in the soft bed.

She did no such thing, and he sensed her pulling herself inward, resisting the carnal urges he caused in her. *She* was the Tigress in control, the mistress of her own desires.

Her gaze darted down to his hardness, at his cock jutting at a painful upright curve from his body. Her appraisal seemed to tell him that he was aroused exactly as she had planned.

"You have an overabundance of *yang*," she said softly. Her voice thrummed sensually through him. "Before you can begin this path, you must be relieved of the excess. Otherwise, you'll feel mad." She slid her touch back to his arms and closed her hands over his shoulder.

"I feel mad now, Lily."

He allowed her to guide him. Her touch was warm and soft, yet firm, and his body sank further into the soft bedding. Arousal hummed along every nerve ending in his skin, culminating in his cock. It throbbed visibly now with the need for release. He panted from the intensity of the pressure. In spite of his avowal to be her student, he wanted desperately in that moment to have her be a soft, pliable woman who would just straddle him, allow him to sheathe his cock deep inside her, and smother him with kisses while she rode them both to bliss.

A smile curved her lips. "I understand. Don't fear. As I have already said, I will help you." She punctuated her promise with the slide of her fingertips up and down the lengths of his thighs. In teasing strokes, she dipped her thumbs down his inner thighs, dangerously close to his erection which twitched with need each time she drew near.

He licked his lips, the juices of his mouth activated by the sight of her hands so close to his cock. He gripped the bedclothes so as not to reach out and pull her closer.

"I will tell you as many times as is necessary," she said gently. "There is nothing wrong with desire." She arched her back, causing her breasts to jut closer to him. She leant in enough to push her nipples against his skin.

He pulled in a breath. "When may I touch you?" he choked out.

She smiled and pressed another soft kiss across his lips. "Soon, Tenzin. After I release some of your excess *yang*."

She moved closer and bent over him. Her nipples brushed his knees, causing him to gasp at the contact; his teeth clenched, and his fingers dug into the bedclothes.

Lily threw her head back, the long hair touching the floor behind her, the movement bringing her nipples closer. Her mouth parted, and she began a sensuous rhythm back and forth, rubbing her hard tips against his knees. She shuddered a few times but never stopped the cadence.

When he thought his seed would spurt out of him, she stopped. Lowering her head, she opened her eyes and gazed at him. Then a small smile curved her lips.

Backing away enough to remove her nipples from contact with him, she grasped his knees with her hands and pushed his legs outward. Inch by inch, she insinuated her body between his legs. The curves of her hips slid against his inner thighs. A shiver ran through his body, and he dug his fingers even deeper into the pillows behind him. It was all he could do not to lunge forward and bring Lily up onto him. The invasion of feminine beauty and scent around him, so close to his skin, was maddening.

He pulled in another deep breath as Lily massaged and caressed his inner thighs. Her hair shimmered blue-black in the lantern light and the sleek fall shifted over her shoulder to hang across one breast. Tenzin stared, captivated by the sight of her dark nipple which peeked out between the strands of her ebony hair. *Gods*, even in his days of indulgence, he hadn't wanted a woman this much.

"Don't worry, Tenzin," she said softly, drawing his attention to the promise in her almond-shaped eyes. "We're almost ready for your release."

# Chapter Five

*The Red Lotus lures the Dragon into the Tigress's mouth. Once the Dragon is captured the Tigress absorbs its* qi. *When the* qi *of the Dragon is absorbed, her spiritual embryo is congealed. This is the meaning of replenishing the* yin *with the* yang.
~Madame Lin from *The White Tigress Manual*

Lily smiled at Tenzin and continued to caress his thigh in light circles. She loved the texture of his skin, and edging closer to his tight, swollen sac caused his breath to tighten even more. His *yang* fire roared now as if it were a blaze in the kitchen hearth. He breathed heavily and he was staring at her hands as they moved over his muscled thighs.

"If you use your desire as a meditation," she went on, "your cravings become a way to the realm of spirit."

She brushed her thumbs along the skin of Tenzin's inner thighs, closer to the plump sac resting at the juncture of his thighs. "Your skin is so smooth here," she said softly.

He pulled in a deep breath and his lips parted. "Thank...thank you, Lily."

His fevered appreciation of her touch and the wonderment mixed with his arousal was a refreshing change and touched something deep inside her. She dared to see that she was enjoying touching this man and breathing deeply of his male scent. A glistening drop of seed seeped from the tip of the dragon's head, and Lily wet her lips in anticipation of tasting him. Tenzin's dragon was thick and veined as it jutted from its nest of dark hair. As it had earlier, the sight made her mouth water, and she worked harder to pace herself, although her *yin* surged, rendering her body completely pliant and ready to receive his *yang*.

Teasingly she slid her fingertips over the underside of Tenzin's *yang* pearls. She traced each plump lobe, appreciating the rougher texture of the skin here than that of his smooth inner thighs. She caressed the crinkled skin and listened to the changes of his breathing as she touched him.

Each intake of his breath grew shallower, and his carved stomach muscles clenched visibly as she made one playful round after the next with the tip of her nail.

She slid the pad of her thumb up the length of his shaft. The reddish golden skin was silky smooth over the hardness. The milky white drop of seed had oozed from the dragon's mouth and now slid downward over the distended length. The scent of that one dragon's tear permeated the air with its muskiness; Lily breathed in the aroma. Tenzin was purer than any other Green Dragon who'd come to her, and his musk stirred her *yin* juices even more.

With a gentle index finger, she swiped the droplet away and tasted it. Her gaze remained on Tenzin's face as she licked.

Oh! Delicious! She suppressed a moan. Salty sweet, like precious nectar. Better than lychee juice. Usually with Green Dragons, she pretended to like the taste of their seed, a ploy to relax them and enhance their sense of manliness so that their *yang* would flow more readily. Her enjoyment now was *no* act, and the need to taste Tenzin's dragon deep in her mouth overwhelmed her.

When she opened her eyes again, Tenzin was staring at her, his dark, velvety eyes wide, as if he'd never imagined she would taste his seed. She smiled gently.

"Your *yang* is so vital," she said. "You are indeed fortunate." She ran a fingertip along a raised vein. "Your blood courses strong in the dragon as it prepares to rear its head."

The sweet tang of the droplet lingered on her tongue long after it had slipped down her throat. Lily averted her gaze from Tenzin's so he wouldn't see her inner struggle. She reached out and closed her hand gently around the stalk of his dragon, leant forward, and engulfed the head between her lips.

Her eyes fluttered closed as Tenzin's cockhead filled her mouth. *Gods*, he tasted as sweet as the essence that had seeped from inside him. She sighed around the plumpness, letting her breath caress Tenzin's thick cock. Her nipples brushed against his knees, heightening her pleasure. *Enjoyment, that's what it was...*

Lowering her head, she took Tenzin's thick dragon in as deeply as she could. He moaned as her lips slid over the silky skin and veins, almost to the base. The sound vibrated in her ears, running in a gentle shiver down her spine and through her limbs. His flesh was delicious, soft and sweet, and she deepened her sucking. The hardness of his erection massaged her tongue and the roof of her mouth, filling her senses better than any food she'd ever tasted.

Time seemed to stop. Her consciousness shrank down to the man in front of her and the pleasure she gave him with her mouth. Appreciation saturated every tiny moan and sigh that came from him. Her own body tingled as she pushed her breasts against his thighs.

She'd entered a flow of giving. The boundary between her body and Tenzin's seemed to melt away, and her mind relaxed, unconcerned with anything else. Tiny lights danced in the blackness that replaced thought, and Tenzin's flavours and sounds, the texture of his dragon against her tongue, the feel of his skin against her nipples, saturated all awareness.

The Place of One Hundred Returnings! She'd reached it! The twinkling lights in her mind were the signpost that had eluded her for so many years. Her heart surged in her chest. For the first time in so very long, her practice seemed to bear fruit. What was more, she felt her former strength begin to seep back into her body. Was it because of Tenzin?

Tenzin. Her attention returned to the man she was pleasuring.

His jade stalk twitched in her mouth. He let out a groan as his hips bucked softly against her rhythm. She held his dragon at its base as his *yang* cloud erupted. She lifted her mouth away and leaned back to give him a clear view of his seed spurting onto her skin, as was the Tigress practice. The milky warmth coated her skin and trickled down her breasts.

When she opened her eyes, Tenzin wasn't watching his ejaculation. His eyes were screwed shut and his head tilted back as he groaned with each spurt of his *yang* cloud. His hands gripped the bedding, and he fell back against the pillows, bracing himself against the force of his climax.

Lily watched him in the throes of release and remained in place so that when he opened his eyes he'd see the erotic sight. He was panting now, eyelids heavy. She released his softening dragon, which rested against one thigh. Moments later, his hands unclenched from the bedding.

For what seemed a long time, she waited, watching Tenzin rise and fall in rhythmic breaths. He lay in this state, seemingly unable to move. She caressed his thighs as she watched his eyelids flutter every few seconds.

She studied him. Sweat gleamed on his golden skin, and his broad chest continued to rise and fall heavily. She began to wonder if he'd fallen asleep. That would be typical. So many men did so after they'd been satisfied. However, in moments, he opened his eyes and lifted his head. His eyes widened as he visibly took in the sight of her, on her knees naked before him, her chest and breasts coated with his seed.

He sat bolt upright. "I'm sorry, Lily. Let me clean you." He leaned over and wiped his hand across her chest.

She grasped his wrist in mid-stroke. "No. It's all right. Enjoy every moment."

"But--"

"This is part of the whole experience. Lie back now." She put gentle pressure on his hand and pushed him back against the pillows, not completely unaware of a strange tickle deep inside her. His responses were so different, so unlike most men's…

He was still watching her, that look of concern in his amber eyes. She worked a smile onto her lips and pushed her breasts out. If she'd been a mortal woman, she would have taken his seed and spread it into the skin of her face. It was a beauty secret she'd shown the Tigresses who applied it every day with the result that they all appeared much younger than they were. However, Lily was immortal, and it made no difference.

She reached for a linen towel and gently wiped herself. Then she returned her attention to Tenzin. His golden skin was flushed, and he sagged back against the pillows, clearly spent. Even so, his dark eyes studied her. "Did you enjoy that, Lily?" he asked softly.

Her gaze whipped to his eyes. She couldn't even remember the last time a man had asked her such a question. She cleared her throat, casting her eyes downward. "I did. Very much."

He continued to look uncertain, and she resisted the impulse to tell him of her spiritual progress. She still didn't know him. He hadn't truly proven himself. "I assure you, Tenzin, I experienced great pleasure."

He bowed his head. "I'm glad." After another moment, he raised his gaze to hers. Renewed desire glazed the deep honey colour of his eyes. "Lily, what about you? I want you to…" his cheeks darkened again and he cleared his throat, "have pleasure."

Lily's heartbeat rose and a sudden nervous perspiration erupted on the back of her neck, like a young girl with a crush. In spite of the excess *yin* that swirled in her body, it was definitely time to send Tenzin to his own sleeping quarters. She didn't like the feeling she had right now. She pushed aside the image of being curled up with him in bed the entire night. A Tigress never spent the night with a Dragon, and it disturbed her that the mere thought had even crossed her mind. Lily stood up and reached for her wrap.

"Come, I'll show you to your room."

Disappointment stabbed Tenzin. After the intimacy they'd just shared, he didn't want to leave her, even for a few hours. He'd been around the entire world searching for his teacher, and now that he'd found her, he wanted only to be near her.

"This is for you." Her voice made him turn, and he saw her holding out a robe.

He took it from her with a bow of his head and slipped it on.

"Your clothing is being laundered," she said. "You will have it back tomorrow.

"Thank you." He watched her slip on her robe and swallowed another stab of disappointment as the material silk covered her body completely.

He followed Lily back out into the courtyard. A soft breeze caressed his face as they padded over the cobbled ground. On the far side of the compound was an open corridor with several doors. Lily pushed open the first one they reached. She looked at him over her shoulder. The glow of the lantern she carried cast shadows on her smooth pretty face.

"This way," she said softly.

She led him into a small room. A cot lined one wall, and a table with one chair filled the main space. The lodgings were simple yet clean and comfortable. Lily set the lantern on the table and turned to him. The expression on her heart-shaped face was unreadable, but Tenzin felt the emotions simmering inside her. "Please remain here until I come for you. Tomorrow I will show you the rest of the compound and explain to you more of what we do here. That is, if you decide to remain."

He bowed his head. "Yes, Lily."

Several moments of silence passed and finally he lifted his gaze to hers. When he did, his breath caught softly. Lily was so beautiful to him, so...perfect. The way the lantern light glowed on her long raven hair and porcelain skin took his breath away. Rationally, he knew that Lily's beauty was not unequalled. Several of the women he'd been with at the House of the Jade Flower were easily as beautiful if not more. But to him, Lily was a wonder.

A look flickered through her violet eyes that made him think she sensed his feelings. She squared her shoulders slightly, and the soft lighting made her silken robe shimmer. "Do you have any questions, Tenzin? You may ask anything, about your practice or about the Temple."

He sensed that the intimacy of the previous hours had helped him pass some sort of test and that Lily found him trustworthy enough to entertain his curiosity. He cleared his throat. "Just one."

"Yes?"

For a brief second, Tenzin almost changed his mind. But his ache for Lily's company spurred him on. "These practices, do they include…" he cleared his throat again and averted his gaze, "consummation?"

"No." The immediacy of her answer made him look up. Lily had narrowed her eyes, and the violet depths flashed. "Absolutely not."

At first the blood in his veins chilled, but another moment of gazing into her eyes, and he understood. Something horrific must have happened to her…

"Do you have a problem with that?" Her voice held a note of panic mixed with anger.

He shook his head. "Of course not, Lily. I just wanted to return the pleasure you gave me."

Lily's eyes widened then narrowed again. She stared at him another moment, and then her expression softened. "When the time comes for you to harvest my *yin*, I will have pleasure. Your concern is most kind." An uncertain look slipped through her beautiful eyes. "Anything else?"

He bowed his head again, wanting so badly to ask her to stay with him, to let him harvest her *yin* now, if it would make her feel as glorious as she'd made him feel. However, the heavens themselves had brought him to Lily. He would have to trust. "No, Lily. Thank you."

She stood in her spot another moment. "Very well. Good night."

Before he could answer, she walked swiftly out.

He watched her leave, drinking in one last glimpse of her hair as it shifted across her back with her movements. Her flowery female scent lingered in the air, as did the memory of her skilled touch and mouth on his body.

Long after she'd left, Tenzin sank down onto his cot. Though he was weary, he folded his legs into the lotus posture and formed a *mudra* with his hands. He spent a long time in meditation before he felt peaceful enough to sleep.

\* \* \* \*

"I can't believe that bitch is here in Shanghai." Wei Yen glared down into the porcelain cup full of scarlet blood in front of her. Not even Zao's large, skilled hands kneading her bare shoulders could ease away her rage. "I wonder how long she's been right under my nose. The whore." Wei Yen took a long sip of blood, then set her cup down.

Zao's hands slid over her shoulders then down across her chest. Usually his touch just above her breasts made her sigh and forget everything else. Not tonight.

Not when she'd just laid eyes on the bitch who'd slain her father then had humiliated her in the underground parlour.

"I lost that hand because of her. Damn her." The Tibetan had probably been a tasty morsel. He'd also had what appeared to be a delicious package hidden under that loincloth. Now she wouldn't know. Fine feeding he'd have made with that sleek, gorgeous body and ripe lips. It was the least the Tan bitch could have done. Cede to her a man in place of one she'd stolen.

Not that there was anything wrong with Zao. Her lover's hands glided again across the tops of her breasts. The tingling warmth of his touch began to penetrate her ire. She let her eyelids flutter and tilted her head back. Yes, Zao kept his mistress's body finely pleasured. When she opened her eyes, she caught a glance of his muscular arm, the golden, flawless skin. Lantern light caught the shine on his long, thick Manchurian queue hanging over his shoulder as he massaged her. He'd made fine feeding too, as a mortal.

Zao remained silent and continued to rub her. He slid his touch closer to her breasts, and a tremor of pleasure shuddered through her, tightening the dark tips. He'd never been a man of words and had proven equally taciturn as a vampire. In this moment, however, she needed succour. "Zao! Say something, dammit!"

Zao's hands stilled on her chest. "Whatever you wish me to do, mistress, I will. You know that."

Wei Yen shot to her feet and paced in front of him, not bothering to pull her wrap closed. "I need you to find that bitch." She covered the length of her bedchamber. The little porcelain butterflies of her hairpiece clinked together as she moved. "Find her. It can't be too difficult. Knowing her, she's probably running a brothel or something like that. The last I'd heard of her she was in Xi'an. She must have been a prostitute or concubine there."

She halted in front of Zao and pierced his gaze. The heat of bloodlust now simmered in her eyes, their greenish glow reflected in her lover's eyes. "Find her, Zao. Find her. And when you do, tell me so I can plan the best way to torment her and make her suffer as she's made me suffer."

She stared a moment longer at Zao. "But don't kill her. She's *my* prize."

"You have my word."

Wei Yen sank back in her chair and motioned for Zao to return to his massage. Zao's fingertips dappled along the sides of her neck then pushed more firmly in sliding strokes. She sighed and closed her eyes, intending to submit to Zao's skilled hands. But seeing Lily Tan again had stirred grief-filled memories, like a stick stirring up the mud from the bottom of a lotus pond. The memory of her mother's screams flooded her mind. She clenched her fists against the memories but was unable to stop the onslaught of grief. She couldn't prevent the vision of her mother's sobbing form bent over her father, a slayer's gleaming knife protruding from his chest.

Wei Yen had been only ten when she saw her father slain. She'd already known he was one of the undead, bitten shortly after Wei Yen's birth, but it hadn't mattered. A daughter didn't care what her father was. She'd loved him anyway.

A large hand covered her shoulder, pressed down with comforting warmth. She opened her eyes and saw that Zao knelt before her. The stirrings of bloodlust glowed in his eyes, too. He picked up her teacup full of blood and held it to her lips. She sipped greedily, imagining it was Lily Tan's blood she drank. She left the last swallow for her lover and held the cup to him.

He took a long drink and set it down. A droplet of blood clung to his bottom lip, stirring her lust. She leaned forward and licked the blood away, eliciting a groan of pleasure from her lover. Her eyelids fluttered as she leant back to savour the coppery taste.

"Don't worry, Wei Yen," she heard Zao say, "I'll take care of it for you."

She nodded, her anger appeased for the moment. Revenge seemed within her grasp. "Good. When it comes time to kill the bitch, I'll do it myself."

# Chapter Six

*When the Green Dragon intermixes with the White Tigress,*
*immortality is achieved.*
~Madame Lin from *The White Tigress Manual.*

*A little girl was screaming. Tenzin saw her from where he looked through the window. She writhed and kicked, struggling like a fish on a line against the two women who tried to hold her down. One woman held the girl's upper body while the second held her legs together and was trying to pull off her little slippers.*

*The girl shrieked and pulled back only to be gripped in place. The second woman yanked off her slippers. A flash of a knife, and the girl screamed as her foot was sliced.*

*Tenzin lunged, tried to pull the girl away, but the people were like shadows slipping through his hands.*

*A woman shrieked. Tenzin's gaze yanked to the girl's foot. The flesh sealed up as they watched, becoming whole, uncut. Both women screamed again, and all arms released the girl. She fell to the floor and scrambled to her feet. The women didn't try to catch her when she darted out of the room.*

*Her cries followed her down the corridor as she slipped into darkness...*

Tenzin opened his eyes and sat bolt upright. His chest heaved as if he'd been the one crying and screaming. His thigh muscles were tight and the soles of his feet burned as if he'd been running.

The images and sounds from his dream spiralled through his mind. His gaze darted this way and that, as if he could spot the little girl in the room's interior. Recollection of the previous evening came back to him: The gaming parlour, beautiful Lily, his new teacher who'd brought him to her chambers and pleasured him. He remembered Lily leading him into the tiny guest room and leaving even though he'd ached to ask her to stay with him.

The dream faded to the background of his consciousness, and as his breathing calmed, he became aware of the soft bedding under his back, the bare walls, and carved screen window that let in fresh summer air, daylight and the sounds of birds in the cherry blossoms of the courtyard.

A light sheen of sweat covered his face and chest, and his armpits felt damp. The memory of the little girl continued to haunt him. Her screams seemed to echo in the still chamber as she struggled to escape the adults who tried to bind her feet. In his recent travels, he'd heard of this custom performed on girls born to wealthy families, of the agony they endured to ensure a good marriage. His heart ached for Lily, for what she'd gone through, for her struggle to free herself. The intensity of her distress made every muscle of Tenzin's body clench.

Yet, her flesh had healed instantly, the hallmark of an immortal. He sighed. Her flesh had healed, but her soul, no doubt, had been scarred.

The only thing he could do was sit and meditate, hoping to diminish the disturbing images before him.

Before he could assume the correct position, a light knock sounded on his door. He threw the covers over his bare groin. "Hello?" His heartbeat rose in anticipation of seeing Lily.

The door opened, and the young woman who'd brought his tea the night before stood there, a tray in her hands and his clothing folded over her arm. She smiled and bowed her head.

He felt a flash of disappointment that it wasn't Lily. and his cheeks heated at being caught undressed.

The girl shuffled in on her bound feet, set the tray on the small table and straightened, avoiding direct eye contact. She was smaller than Lily, but emitted the same sense of delicate strength. The pink silk blouse she wore contrasted enticingly with her pale skin and waist-length hair.

"Mistress Lily is with the others," she said in a quiet voice. "They do their exercises each morning." She paused, her gaze towards the floor. "She wanted me to give you your clothing and…this." With a graceful wave of her hand, she indicated a small scroll on the tray, next to the teapot and bowls of food. Then she set his vest and pants over the back of the chair.

"Mistress Lily said you need to discharge more excess *yang* before she sends for you today." The woman looked back up at him. Her dark eyes shone, and her skin glowed. She was the picture of vibrant health. "I am to help you, if you wish." She bowed her head again in practiced modesty.

Tenzin's heart skidded a bit. "He-help…me?"

She nodded, still averting his gaze. Apparently, modesty was supposed to be alluring. "Yes. I will bring forth the dragon's cloud with my touch, if you so desire."

Sudden heat curled through his groin and sweat broke out in his armpits. He pulled the bedclothes closer over his growing erection. This girl was beautiful and radiated warmth and passion, but he wished again that Lily had been standing there. If she had been, he would have already pulled aside the covers and asked for her next instruction.

"You're not obliged to accept," the girl said. "The practice can be done in solitude."

Relief prickled through his skin. He let out a breath and bowed. "Thank you."

A shy smile curved her full, dusky lips, though a look akin to disappointment flashed through her dark eyes. She did not, to his distinct relief, appear offended. "You may call on me if you need anything." She bowed her head again and retreated before he could say anything else.

When she'd gone, he threw back the cover, dashed over, grabbed the scroll, and recovered himself, as if Fei Liu might return any second. Waiting an extra moment, he carefully unrolled the parchment, catching his breath at the unexpected contents. Drawings showed a man, naked, his penis large and hard, the shaft resting in his hand. The successive drawings showed the stages of self-pleasure, all the way to the release of his seed. In spite of his own excessive experiences, Tenzin felt colour flush his cheeks.

The man in the erotic sketches sat, reclined on a bed, legs bent, the soles of his feet pressed together. His eyes were closed, and arrows demonstrated that he took a deep breath with each stroke of his hand.

After one last check at his window to assure he was alone, Tenzin pulled back the covers and assumed the position indicated in the scroll. He closed his eyes and pictured Lily.

Immediately, he felt himself harden.

His breathing deepened as he pictured her violet eyes, her smooth pale skin, and firm breasts. He remembered the way her glossy, ebony hair had sifted across her back and brushed his bare thighs, the willowy curve of her waistline when he'd spanned it with his hands, and the tiger tattoo covering her pale skin and bare sex. He relived the way her mouth had felt on his cock, the way she'd massaged the hard shaft with her lips, swirled her tongue over the head and sucked the droplets that seeped from him. Dragon's tears, she'd called them. She'd known just how hard or soft to suckle—even bite—him. Her giving nature had come through in the passionate yet measured way she'd pleasured him, as if she'd been holding back on her own fulfilment in order to maximize his.

Energy flowed freely through his body now; sexual need tingled and pulsed in his dragon and made his balls tighten and swirl with fullness. His breathing became shallow and more rapid.

His hand felt warm and smooth against his fully hard shaft. He remembered the way Lily had knelt before him like a high priestess before a shrine and taken his *likpa* into her delicate hand. She had touched him with such care and tenderness with both her hands and mouth, as if his phallus were the most precious object. It was this sweet pleasure that inspired him to deepen the strokes against himself now.

The first slide of his palm along his cock made his breath hitch. He paused, telling himself to breathe deeply, in rhythm with his hand. Perhaps to direct the *yang* flow, but his mind refused to focus.

With his other hand, he cupped his sac and squeezed it gently in small circles the way the scroll had instructed.

The thought of Lily's mouth around his male stem filled his mind. He stroked. Breathed. Stroked again. Squeezed.

In his vision, Lily's head had bobbed up and down as she swallowed him deeply in her mouth and slid back up again.

Tingling energy intensified in his cock, swirled rapidly in his balls. So many times he'd done this, alone, where no one could hear him or see him. But now, something was different...more real...alive and vivid. He thought of Lily and felt a connection to her. It was as if she were there in the room with him, her energy mingling with his.

He stroked harder. Breathed harder. Squeezed a bit harder. Pleasure shimmered all around the shaft of his cock and in his balls. Wherever his palms touched, sparks of pleasure showered him.

Several short, hard bursts of energy pulsated in his shaft. He sucked in his breath and stiffened. His eyes squeezed shut, and the warm moisture of his seed shot out, coating his hands. Energy continued to pulsate, tingle, and flow, draining bit by bit. He tilted his head back and groaned softly with the release of pressure. Slowly, he became aware again of the room, the birds in the courtyard trees, the breeze rustling the leaves, the sound of soft footfalls Another knock on his door...

His eyes flew open.

"Tenzin--" Lily's voice sounded through the door. "--don't move. I must check you."

His heart gave a small flipping sensation. He'd wanted to see Lily so much, and now her sudden presence made him anxious.

"Yes," he called out softly. His chest heaved, the soles of his feet remained pressed together, and he rested in the same position, breathless, his hand still circling his now relieved cock. "Come in."

Lily wiped her palm against her silk trouser leg, amazed at how damp her skin felt. For some unaccountable reason, she was nervous. There was no reason she should be. How many countless times had she examined a Dragon's ejaculate for his *yang* quality?

Was her pulse quickening because deep in her abdomen she felt a growing need to reach that place of exultation she'd reached last night? She swallowed, already feeling weak in the knees at the mere thought of the pulsating Tenzin inspired in her *yin* pearl. Her hand trembled as she pushed open his door.

*Pull yourself together, Lily.* It would not do to behave like an adolescent girl just discovering men. Or, at least, what she *imagined* the discovery of sexual titillation felt like for a pubescent female. Her own initiation had been gruesome, horrible, at a vampire's hands and fangs. Xu Yu, a monster in human guise.

Only an immortal's slaying knife had ended his filthy reign over her body and soul.

Perhaps her nervousness was due more to that fact that Tenzin had appeared in her dreams last night. She'd fallen right to sleep after she'd left him, more relaxed than she'd felt in a long time despite her imbalance of *yin*. Her sleep had been a deep, dreamless one, until just before waking. He'd watched her, a little girl writhing and struggling in her mother's and auntie's grips. They'd tried to slice open her feet, induce the infection that would soften the bones, make them pliable so her feet could be bound. Tenzin's eyes had radiated compassion. He'd reached out, tried to stop the women, but couldn't touch her...

Lily blinked away the memory of his compassionate face in her dream. She dragged in a deep breath and walked in.

Tenzin was there, naked, on his cot. Sweat glistened on his golden muscles. His chest rose and fell heavily, and small puddles of his thick *yang* cloud shone on his stomach and chest. His dragon, half hard, lay against one thick, muscular thigh.

A shudder of desire cascaded through her body. With practiced control, however, she crossed the small room and bent over him. He remained in the position shown on the scroll she'd sent, knees bent, the soles of his feet pressed together. The scent of his dragon's cloud filled the room, roused her hunger for him.

"I did what you instructed, Lily."

She nodded. "I see." She reached out, gathered some of his seed off his stomach and tested it between her fingertips. The substance was definitely thinner than the evening before. She looked again at his face. His eyes were clearer this morning, less charged with hunger, and he breathed with greater stillness. His *yang* was definitely more balanced, and he was ready to harvest some of her *yin*.

She reached for the cloth she'd included on the tray, wet it in a nearby wash basin, and knelt in front him. With gentle strokes, she wiped him clean. Fei Liu must have serviced him well, but she'd failed to clean Tenzin's seed from his body. A tickle of jealousy nagged her. "Where is Fei Liu? Did she not help you discharge your *yang*?"

"I was grateful for her willingness to assist me," Tenzin said, "but I declined." He looked straight into Lily's eyes, his expression even. "I'm sorry if I offended your hospitality. To be honest..." he paused and cleared his throat, "...I want to practice only with *you*."

Her fingers tightened on the cloth, bracing her against the sudden reaction of her *yin*. It softened, intensifying her already strong response to his male beauty.

He blinked and bowed his head. Colour bloomed in his smooth cheeks. "I'm sorry," he said. "You're the teacher. I'm the student. I've no right to—"

"No, it's all right." The words were out before she realised what she'd said. She heard her own even tone, an almost flat sound that completely concealed the flush of ridiculous pleasure his request gave her. She blinked again and swallowed. Nervousness made her throat feel thick.

She hadn't realised until that moment how for granted she'd taken it that Tenzin would let Fei Liu service him. It had never occurred to her for even a moment that he would refuse such a beautiful Tigress as Fei Liu. She appeared to be a young woman of eighteen or nineteen, but her devotion to the Tigress practices had restored her youth, belying her thirty-six years.

Lily glanced away from Tenzin and distracted herself with cleaning his skin. Truthfully, she wanted nothing more than to have him discharge her *yin*. She hadn't intended to let him touch her this morning, yet his request for her exclusive touch made her feel…sweet. No man had ever made such a request of her before. The Green Dragons who let her Tigresses harvest their *yang* didn't seem particular about which woman suckled them or touched them. "You've done nothing wrong. If you wish only to practice with me, that is fine."

Tenzin sat up and leaned in towards her. Those fathomless eyes of his gazed out at her with warmth. "Thank you, Lily."

She stared back at him a moment longer, trembling. Her jade gate had already begun to open, to expose the delicate *yin* pearl that no man had touched for so long. Dare she trust him with her most vulnerable part? For a brief second, it occurred to her that maybe she *should* have him work with Fei Liu. But she dismissed the thought almost immediately, surprised with the rapid surge of possessiveness she felt.

"It's time to continue our practices," she murmured before she could change her mind. Tenzin had passed a test that she hadn't even intended to give him. She rose and set aside the cloth. Turning to face the bed again, she began to undo the top frog closure of her blouse.

She watched Tenzin's Adam's apple move up and down as she proceeded to the next closure. Slowly she continued down the front of her blouse until it lay open. She felt more confident now, sure of her powers. Slipping her fingers between the crack, she pushed the opening wider so that the cloth half-covered her bound breasts. She licked her lips at the sensation growing between her legs.

Tenzin's eyes were fastened on her fingers.

"Would you like to see more?" she asked him in a husky whisper.

Slowly, he nodded, his Adam's apple once again bobbing.

Lily gave him a teasing smile and let the blouse fall open. She didn't usually make such a show of undressing, but she couldn't help wanting to prolong the appreciative, wide-eyed awe reflected in his eyes as he watched. Just as slowly, teasingly, she unhooked her trousers and let them fall. She stepped out of them and toed off her slippers.

Warmth flushed her cheeks. With a slow, languid movement, she unwrapped the binding cloth around her breasts until they sprang free. She dropped the cloth aside, moved her hands to her breasts and palmed them, then proceeded downward, smoothing her palms over her ribcage and belly and over her hips, her eyes all the while on Tenzin's reaction. To her great pleasure, sweat beaded on his brow, and his mouth hung open. She suppressed a chuckle, not wanting to sound crude. He didn't know the teasing wasn't part of the practice, but something she did because he was such an appreciative audience.

She perched on the bed and slid closer. "You're going to need to know the language of our practice," she said.

"Teach me," he said, his voice barely a whisper.

"I will." Wanting to prolong the admiration a bit longer, she proceeded to take the pins from her hair, then shoved her fingers into the thick bundle and loosened it from its confinement. She shook her head and felt her locks tumble around her shoulders. She arched her head back, allowing her mane to caress her back and tickle her buttocks, knowing all the while what an enticing picture she presented.

With a final shake of her hair, she drew in a deep breath, her breasts jutting forward with the intake of air. "As you already know, the female is the *yin* half of our human life force, and the male is *yang*."

She bent one knee on the bed and sank down beside Tenzin's body. "This is your dragon." So saying, she reached out and brushed her fingertips along his semi-flaccid shaft. In response, his member twitched, and his stomach drew in with a sharp intake of breath.

She paused against the flood of *yin* in her own body. Touching this man was truly a delight she hadn't known in so long. "The fluid that comes forth from it has several names." As she spoke, she brushed her fingertips over the head. "The droplets that seep out before ejaculation are called dragon's tears." Her thumbpad rubbed softly over the small cleft of its opening. "The pool of it is your *yang* cloud." She slid her touch lower and circled the swells of his testicles with the pads of her fingertips. Tenzin's pelvis shifted on the mattress. "These are your *yang* pearls. Any questions about that?" She looked at his face as her fingers gently deepened their pressure on his sac.

Tenzin shook his head.

"You are speechless?"

His only response was to swallow. His dark eyes shifted from her face downward. The way she was leaning forward, she knew her breasts fell forward, suspended over him. She could feel the heat of his desire curl in her own belly. She turned completely to him and rose slightly on her knees. She smiled when his gaze shifted downward. He seemed fascinated by her tattoo, especially the tigress's belly.

She sat back and spread her thighs apart slightly, one leg partly over his. "There are many names for the woman's intimate parts," she said, feeling the heat burn again in her cheeks. Explaining these terms to Tenzin was a far different matter than teaching it to her Tigress cubs. "However, you need to know only a few. The jade gate." Reaching down to her lower lips, she spread them.

Another curl of heat travelled through her belly down into her sex. She slid her fingers over the tiny hooded nub. It tingled under her touch.

"The *yin* pearl," she said. "It is this spot that holds the key to both partners' enlightenment. So much *qi*, life force, concentrates here that it is a vital part of the practice."

Tenzin's gaze was locked on her open sex. He had raised himself on his elbows. His lips were slightly parted, and his chest heaved. Lily paused under his worshipful look. The way he stared at her intimate parts made her feel that he would never find anything wrong with them. She pushed her index finger inside her opening, restraining the gasp of pleasure. Hopefully, it would be his fingers causing the ripple of pleasure her own touch gave.

Tenzin leant forward ever so slightly. "May I?" he asked softly, his own hand coming forward.

The nearness of his eager hand sent another ripple of *qi* through her lower body. She wanted nothing more than to let him touch her, but couldn't. A Tigress always maintained control.

"In a moment," she said.

# Chapter Seven

*Where the Green Dragon must retain, the White Tigress must absorb.*
*Where the Green Dragon seeks tranquillity, the White Tigress seeks*
*activity.*
~Madame Lin from *The White Tigress Manual*

"This is the jade cave," Lily continued. The friction of her own finger inside her while Tenzin watched stirred her *yin* to liquid heat. Feeling her cheeks burn, she slid her finger out, barely recognising the lustful creature inside her who threatened to drown out her Tigress's control. "Now, sit against the wall and open your legs."

Tenzin nodded and scooted to the head of the bed, his fervent gaze never leaving her body.

That ridiculous flush of pleasure his silent admiration gave her spread through her once again. Gathering her hair into a quick knot at the nape of her neck, she suppressed a girlish smile and positioned herself in front of him, her back pressed lightly to his chest. The touch of his bare flesh to hers was pleasurable, and she resisted the urge to sink against him. She turned slightly. "What we're going to do is bring forth my *yin* and then, when I'm ready, you will release it from me and draw it into yourself. This will help balance both of us. Give me your hands."

Tenzin raised his arms on either side of her. The warm, masculine strength he exuded surrounded her, and she shuddered with the pleasure of it.

She grasped his wrists and brought his obedient hands to her breasts. "With the lightest touch possible, you'll circle my breasts seventy-two times in each direction. By the time you've finished, my yin should have risen enough for you to harvest. Like this." She moved Tenzin's hands over her breasts. The callused flesh of his palms rubbed the swells of flesh, and she felt her *yin* surge. "Do you understand?"

"Yes, Lily." Tenzin's voice was husky, and she could feel his hands tremble.

She released his wrists and took a deep breath. "All right. Then begin."

Tenzin leaned in closer to her, and his dragon, now fully hard, pushed into the crevice of her buttocks. Another pleasant shudder passed through her, and she sagged against him a bit more. Tenzin began the circling she'd shown him, and his whisper light touch grazed her breasts, tapping her nipples with each round. Icy heat ignited in her breasts and spread through her belly. Her jade cave, already moist, grew slippery, seeping with *yin* dew more on each round.

Tenzin had barely begun the exercise, and her body already demanded release. His breath was warm on her skin, pulsing lightly onto the curve of her neck. His life force, potent and male, swirled in the air and made his musky scent fill her senses.

Without meaning to, Lily let her eyes flutter closed and tilted her head back, letting it rest against him. This brought her breasts closer to his fingers. His circles grew harder until he cupped the swells in his palm and kneaded her hardening nipples with the flats of his hands. He wasn't supposed to touch so closely, but Lily found she couldn't...didn't want...to correct him. After so long, a gentle man's touch was irresistible. There would time enough to correct him later, when she had been balanced.

His hands lightly squeezed her breasts. The warm, male energy around them whirled into her body. She grasped the bedclothes and curled her fingers harshly into them. She was determined for Tenzin to finish the seventy-two rounds in each direction even though she was ready now for release. The way he was touching her had made her *yin* surge hotter and faster than she'd intended.

Tenzin pressed his lips to her neck and feathered the tip of his tongue over her quivering flesh.

Her resolve slipped.

"Tenzin," she breathed, "I'm ready now." She grasped his hands and turned around, manoeuvred her body so that they sat facing each other, and she straddled his hips. "First, drink my *yin* through our kiss and then through my breasts."

"Yes, Lily." Tenzin leaned forward, cupped her cheeks and pressed his lips to hers.

The kiss was so soft, so gentle that Lily felt herself melt. Her lips fell open, and Tenzin's breath pulsed softly into her mouth. She could feel him drink in her essence, felt the soft, peaceful flow of *qi* between them. In the next heartbeat, she slipped her tongue between his lips and brushed it against his. He responded in kind and danced his tongue against hers, following the rhythm she made.

She slid her hands from his cheeks down his chest and around to his back. Without thinking, she sank down, against the pillows.

With their mouths still pressed together, Tenzin followed her, his chest pressed to her breasts, his legs straddling her hips. Pulling his lips from hers, Tenzin rained a trail of soft kisses over her chin, dappled his lips over her throat and chest. Tingling heat ignited in her skin wherever his kiss touched her skin.

He closed his lips over one hard nipple and tugged it gently against his tongue.

Lily moaned softly. She clasped her hands around his head. His hair brushed her fingertips pleasantly, and the twinkling lights pulsated gently in her mind as her body filled with ecstasy.

Lily's sweet, dark nipple pebbled under Tenzin's tongue. The light, musky flavour of the tight bud rolled on his taste buds, making his mind feel like it was melting away. He loved the way she clasped his head and arched her back, pushing her breast deeper into his mouth. Suddenly, he felt her raise her legs. In the next second, her supple inner thighs pushed into his hips, and the heels of both her feet pressed into his backside. He could swear she was drawing him closer, and he answered by sinking down onto her inviting softness. His cock, fully hard to the point of throbbing, brushed her pelvic bone.

With one hand, he caressed her other breast, kneaded the nipple to hardness between his fingertips. With his other, he reached down between her thighs to the tigress's belly, that deeply intimate part of Lily that fascinated and compelled him. He slid his fingertips over the smooth, fleshy lips and ventured between the folds.

Lily moaned softly and tilted her pelvis against his hand. Her yin juices seeped freely from her sex, and the intoxicating scent diffused into the air.

He coated his fingertips with her musk and rubbed it over her pearl in light, quick strokes.

Lily's body shuddered in response. She sighed and arched her back in what felt like a silent demand.

Suddenly her thighs tightened on his hips. "Tenzin, stop."

The pressure of her hands on his shoulder made him still on her breast. He lifted his face up. "Am I hurting you?"

She shook her head. "No, but you must harvest the *yin* correctly. Do only to me what I did for you last night. Only that."

He studied Lily's violet eyes, they were tinged with sensual desire, but there was something else in them too, something that hung on the last two words she'd said. *Only that.*

She rose up on her elbows, watching him. Her beautiful face was flushed and her lips swollen from their kiss. "Is this something you wish to do, Tenzin?"

The scent of her *yin* musk rose in the air, making it hard to concentrate on his train of thought, but he managed to nod. "Very much so."

She smiled and scooted back, towards the pillow so that he knelt between her thighs. "You can stay on the bed or kneel down on the floor. As you wish."

He cleared his throat. His mouth watered at the mere suggestion of tasting her so intimately. "Here is fine, Lily." Without another word, he lowered himself down, so close her female scent invaded him. The soft folds of her sex invited his touch, and a mere glance at it showed her dew glistening within.

"Please, taste me now," she said, her voice a breathy whisper.

Her words made his insides jump. With a touch as light as a flower petal, he slid his fingertips down her belly. He heard her breath catch, and her stomach caved and rose again under his fingertips. Slowly, gently he traced the contours of the leaping tiger, starting with the claws over her ribs. The fascinating colours had done nothing to mar the soft perfection of her skin, which felt to him softer than downy feathers.

He flattened his palm over her smooth belly, covering the tiger's shoulder and deepening the kneading of her skin. Her breath hitched, and he glanced at her. "Too hard?"

"No, oh. Keep doing that." Her words came out breathless.

She encircled one of his wrists and stopped his motion when he reached the gentle slope of her breasts. She began to move his hand downward. "Do what I did…to you," she repeated.

"I will," he said, resisting the pressure on his wrist and bringing his hand back up to the rise of her breast. "I just had to touch you some more."

His cock tightened, grazing her leg as he moved his body upward. She finally let his wrists go, and he was free to do what he'd been dying to do since he'd glimpsed her dusky nipples through her sheer robe. As if he were a priest at a shrine, he bowed over her twin breasts, and brought his palms against each side.

Again, he resumed the gentle kneading until he could sense her relaxing once more against the pillow. Like a hummingbird over a flower, he let his thumbpads hover over her nipples, touching and retreating, touching and retreating, as his warm palms rubbed circles over her breasts, until the aureoles wrinkled and the peaks hardened.

"Yesss..." Her back arched, pushing her nipples closer to his thumbs even as she shook her head back and forth. "Oh...no — oh," she moaned and lifted higher.

He lifted his head. Her nipples were hard, taut, reaching up to him. He closed his mouth again over one and suckled it. She whimpered and tilted up to him. Her sweet flavour fuelled his need to taste her *yin* pearl. He retreated and rained kisses down the centre of her stomach, over her belly button, and lower.

He smoothed one hand over her inner thigh, his forehead resting on her soft stomach. Never had he felt skin so silky. Her scent wafted up to his nostrils as he lowered his face to her tiger's belly. Lily's smooth mound was as soft as a flower petal. He sank lower on his knees to concentrate his attention on what lay beneath. Her fleshy lower lips were open, revealing the soft pink contours of her inner sex. Tenderly, he ran the pad of his thumb down the moist centre and felt her body quiver in response. He brought his finger up to his mouth and tasted her dew.

Her breathing deepened, and the husky sound filled his ears. He caressed the soft skin of her thigh again, loving the dusky pale gold tone that contrasted with the darker hue of his own skin.

Closing his eyes, he brushed his lips across a spot on her inner thigh. She released a quick breath, and the scent of her *yin* juices surged, hot and potent. He kissed the spot again, lingered this time, and trailed soft kisses upward, closer to her sex.

With gentle thumbs, he spread the fleshy lips wider and pressed his mouth to the small, hooded nub at her core. He'd learned long ago that when this part of a woman was properly touched, it brought her to bliss. And he fully intended to do that to Lily.

Lily's breath, though still soft, panted more rapidly. He swiped his tongue lightly across her clit, and then blew on it.

She released a sigh and from the corner of his eye, he saw her long-nailed hands clutch the bed sheets.

He held her sex open and licked her *yin* pearl gently with tiny strokes of his tongue, up and down, around the small nub.

Lily was nearly breathless. The sight of Tenzin's dark head between her thighs blurred, and she panted. Tenzin was obviously skilled in the ways of a woman's body, and he seemed determined to show her just how much so. She thought she'd die from the pleasure when he'd sucked her breasts, but that was nothing compared to what he was doing now.

The moist warmth of his tongue descended on her *yin* pearl again, stroking the sensitive flesh until she could only throw her head back and stare upward into the shadows. She tightened her grip on the bedclothes and tried not to thrust her sex down, demanding the release he was coaxing from her.

Her nipples, hardened to tight peaks, tingled, a sensation directly connected to the waves of pleasure travelling through her from Tenzin's mouth.

Tenzin shifted, moved one hand, then pushed a finger through her jade gate. She sucked in a breath. He was being so careful, filling her passage so gradually, as if she were a virgin. He licked her pearl again, teasing it with tiny licks of his tongue while he pulsed the finger in and out of her in gentle strokes.

She moaned and writhed on the bed. Her eyelids fluttered as the room seemed to darken, and those tiny lights she'd seen before twinkled again in her consciousness.

Her body unclenched, and she felt the tingling energy pass from Tenzin's mouth and hand into her. The energies swirled together and gathered swiftly in her core. She felt as if she were floating even as the tension mounted.

Tenzin sucked her faster now. His tongue flickered over her pearl with a more fevered rhythm, and his finger worked up a friction of heat inside her. He closed his lips over her inner sex and tightened them.

The tiny lights expanded and shimmered. Time seemed to stop as waves of bliss ploughed through her sex. She shuddered and cried out, not recognising the voice as her own. Her hips rose up to meet Tenzin's mouth, as her sex craved more and more of the release only he could give her. He responded by grabbing her buttocks in his hands and pressing his tongue deeper into her opening.

The waves mounted and crested, mounted and crested, as every inch of her consciousness centred around her core.

One last whimper of sheer pleasure and her body collapsed into the mattress, wilted as a jade plant left in the sun for too long. She could barely breathe, her mind consumed with the intensity of sensations that had rocked her body. Tenzin's hands remained on her bottom, and he stroked her skin lightly with his thumbs.

She let him remain quietly like that, resting on her as she recuperated.

She could do nothing else but gaze up at the ceiling, her mind too dazed to form cohesive thoughts. All she could concentrate on was how intense, how uplifting the experience she'd just had had been. It was as if every light in the universe had exploded inside her and now only gradually was her body putting itself back together again.

She felt Tenzin shift, and she lifted her head an inch, the motion almost too much effort. His dark eyes gleamed with desire. Her yin dew coated his lips and chin. He looked wild and predatory. "Did I please you, Lily?"

There was no mockery in his voice, only a simple humility. She stared at him. He had had mastery over her for those minutes, and yet there he lay, his gaze open and honest, asking if he had pleased her. Speech was difficult, but his seeming rawness compelled her to answer. "More than words could say."

"And I didn't hurt you in any way?"

*Hurt her?* Lifting her head, she stared at him. Her eyes took a moment to focus and when they did, she clearly read the uncertainty in his eyes. Without thinking, she reached out and brushed a fingertip across his damp cheek. For the second time in less than a day's time, she'd experienced the Place of One Hundred Returnings. Until Tenzin, she had thought her Tigress practice to be completely in vain.

"It was…beautiful," she managed in a broken whisper.

She was unprepared for the smile that met her praise. The uncertainty left his eyes, and they filled with warmth. His full lips curved upward, and he bowed his head. "Thank you, my teacher."

The gratitude in his expression and in his voice made her heart flutter. She levered herself up to a sitting position and patted the spot beside her. "Come."

He rolled over and pushed himself up to her, giving her a clear view of his renewed desire, evident in the hard upward curve of his erection. And yet, he asked for nothing, seeming content just to be with her. She cupped his cheek. The scent of her own musk clung to his face, a stark reminder of the bliss Tenzin had given her moments ago. She leant forward, tilted her head back and pressed her lips to his.

He let out a small breath, as if surprised that she'd kissed him, but in the next moment parted his lips. Their breath mingled in the warmth of each other's mouths, and again, Lily saw the twinkling of lights. His male scent filled her, mixed with her own tangy *yin*. He moaned softly, and she sensed he would not ask for release but would wait for her to show him the next step.

With her lips to his, she reached for his dragon, closed her hand lightly around the thick shaft, and stroked it, light quick caresses that brought him rapidly to a second climax. His *yang* cloud shot out and coated his stomach and her hand. With her other hand, she cupped the back of his neck, keeping their mouths together while she stroked his emptying dragon.

Only then did she break their kiss, letting her hand remain on his neck.

She watched his heavy dark eyelashes flutter and listened to the hard rasp of his breath.

"Let me wipe you," he said in a breathy voice when he'd recovered.

She smiled at him, charmed again by his desire to please her. "No need. Watch." She gathered up a dollop of his dragon's tears and smoothed it into her cheek.

Tenzin's eyes widened.

She chuckled. "It's a beauty secret of the Tigress sect. Many of the women you'll meet here are much older than you would believe them to be. As much from doing this as from balancing their *qi*."

A look of boyish wonder lit his features. "Is that true, Lily?"

She nodded and massaged a bit more into her other cheek. It didn't matter that she, herself, didn't need the stuff to stay looking younger, but if this would ease Tenzin's shame about his own fluids, so be it. "I swear it's true."

He smiled again, that radiant smile she found beautiful. "Well, then I don't feel so bad."

She reached for the towel she'd used earlier and wiped the excess, both from her hand and off his torso. "Never feel bad about your *yang* force, Tenzin."

He averted her gaze. "I'm sorry you need to repeat that. I wish I could simply understand."

Would that all men had Tenzin's humility. "You will understand in time. The most important lessons take the longest to learn."

Her words were met with a grateful smile.

"Mistress Lily! Mistress Lily, come quick! It's Jade! *He's* here!" Fei Liu's voice was just outside the room.

A chill travelled down Lily's spine. Without thinking, she grasped Tenzin's shoulder. "Jade's husband. He's found her. I must go!"

# Chapter Eight

*Where the Green Dragon must be passive, the White Tigress must be aggressive. Like the two fish of the t'ai chi, each must seek after its opposite to be complete.*
~Madame Lin from *The White Tigress Manual*

Tenzin vaulted off the bed after Lily. He threw on his clean clothes as Lily dressed, noticing she did not take the time needed to rewrap her breasts.

"It was only a matter of time 'til he found her." Lily didn't seem to be addressing him directly, but he heard the fear that saturated her voice. She'd barely pushed her feet into her slippers, and she was out the door.

Tenzin followed on her heels through the courtyard, into the greeting area, and out the front door. He furrowed his brow as he followed her down the quiet street to the main thoroughfare. Where could they possibly be going?

She turned into the first brothel on the corner. As soon as they stepped into the dark coolness of the place, furnished in an array of red silk cushions and heavy carved furniture, a woman's screams punctuated by the sounds of a hand slapping flesh echoed from the back.

"You whore!" a man shouted.

"Stop! Tzan Ru! Stop! Please!" the woman screamed.

In the next second, a huge man with the physique of a fighter appeared, his long Manchurian queue swinging against his back. In one beefy hand, he clutched a long fall of ebony hair. One powerful yank and the rest of the screaming, half-dressed woman slid through the same doorway, arms flailing.

"Tzan Ru, let her go!" Lily lunged towards him.

Tenzin grasped her shoulder, but she yanked from his grip and ran down the hall. Reaching the man she'd called Tzan Ru, she delivered a sharp, precise kick to one leg.

She might as well have kicked a stone wall. Lily stepped back, raised one arm, and delivered a chop to his side. Tzan Ru grunted and dropped Jade. Several other women crowded around her and pulled the crying woman back into the room.

Tzan Ru turned to Lily. Anger glazed his wide, flat face. He thrust a pointed finger at her. "You're the Tigress bitch that stole my wife!"

He raised his fist, but Tenzin flashed forward and caught the meaty hammer before it could land on Lily. "You must leave now," Tenzin growled. "No violence against a woman will be tolerated here."

The man, nearly a head taller than Tenzin, glowered at him. He yanked his fist from Tenzin's grasp. "I have a right. That bitch stole my wife and made a whore of her. I'm taking her back where she belongs." He lunged at Tenzin, fist raised again.

Like lightning, Lily stepped in and jostled Tenzin aside. To Tenzin's surprise, she bowed her head, appearing suddenly submissive. "If it is a matter of finances, honoured sir, I will purchase Jade from you at whatever price you demand. Certainly a man of your stature can procure a higher quality wife, perhaps even a woman with bound feet."

Tzan Ru glared at Lily, but Tenzin saw immediately that the mention of money had caught his attention. "One hundred *yuan*," he muttered. "No less."

Tenzin's gaze whipped to Lily at the steep price. But she didn't flinch.

"Done. Tenzin, remain here with Mr. Chen while I retrieve his funds." Lily gave Tenzin a pointed look.

Tenzin nodded, keeping a guarded eye on Tzan Ru while Lily disappeared to the rear of the place. The huge man crossed his arms and stared straight ahead in the dusky hallway with the women's sniffles in the background. His tension radiated in the air, and Tenzin felt his own body tense, ready to fight him should he change his mind and go at Jade, who was only a few feet away inside the nearest room.

Lily returned momentarily with a small pouch in one hand. The clink of coins tinkled with each step she made. In front of Tzan Ru, she opened the pouch. "One hundred *yuan*, as agreed upon, more than enough to purchase the finest bred of wives."

Tenzin looked from the pouch, to Lily's even expression, to Tzan Ru.

"I apologise for your distress, Mr. Chen," Lily went on, obviously not giving Tzan Ru a chance to find an argument. "I have scolded Jade in the past about her abandonment of so noble a husband, but she refused to listen. However, I am a business woman and could not turn away an eager worker." She bowed her head again. "That is my fault completely."

Tzan Ru fixed her with a look of disgust. Tenzin could practically hear the words of insult he wanted to shower on Lily, but he also saw Lily had put Tzan Ru into a position where to act further in a violent manner would brand him as the man of lower class and intelligence that he was. A wave of admiration for Lily's wit, courage, and strength swept through Tenzin.

A meaty hand came out and closed around the pouch. "I will not deign to set foot in this place again." He spat on the ground.

Lily bowed her head. She was the vision of a perfectly submissive woman, only she'd taken complete control of the situation. "As you wish, honoured sir. Tenzin, escort our guest out."

"Yes, mistress."

Tzan Ru stalked down the hall. Tenzin followed him to the doorway, making sure he actually left. He watched Tzan Ru disappear around the corner and then went back in.

He found Lily in the Jade's room, kneeling before the crying woman. The room around them was in shambles, pillows strewn, clothing in rumpled heaps on the floor. Jade's face paint was smeared around the swelling and bruising, and her hair went in all different directions like some sort of crazy fan.

Lily cupped one tearstained cheek. "He won't be back, Jade. I promise." She dabbed a wet cloth onto a cut. "You must not let this hinder your goal of Immortality. Continue to harvest yang and go about your business. All right?"

Jade nodded through her sniffles. "Thank you, Mistress Lily."

Lily handed the cloth to a woman nearby. "Ye Cao, tend to her, please." She rose up on her knees and placed a soft kiss on Jade's forehead. "Clean up and restore order here," she said to the three other women who remained huddled close to Jade.

Lily looked at another girl. "Ming, where was Fen Chow through all this?"

The woman she'd addressed bowed her head. "Drunk. He fell asleep in the back."

Tenzin expected Lily's anger, but to his surprise, she sighed. "Make him some tea, sober him up, and don't discharge his *yang* for at least a week."

Lily turned to leave. She reached the doorway then halted. Perhaps she had a better use for Fen Chow's expended state. Now was the perfect opportunity to show the beginner's class how an experienced Tigress harvested a man's *yang*. "On second thought, clean him up. I have a task for him."

Ming bowed her head again. "Yes, Mistress Lily."

"I will wait here and help you," Lily added. Certainly they would need an immortal's physical strength to carry a man of Fen Chow's bulk, even a short distance. She meant to go with the girl and help but sagged back suddenly against the wall. Tzan Ru's yang lingered in the hall, and now she experienced the weakening effect his bile had actually had on her, as well as from her own aggression, kicking and chopping at him. There had been a time such activity and driving life force would not have affected her this way, but now, even with Tenzin's *yang* to help her...

Tenzin. Lily suddenly remembered his quiet presence in the hallway. She went out to where he stood, yet found herself unable to look at him. She didn't want to see his expression, risk finding judgement there. It was a fault of hers that she did often care what others thought of her, she just didn't let her concern show or let it stop her from working with her Tigresses.

Even though Tenzin had helped her defend Jade from Tzan Ru, he'd also learned about an aspect of her school that appeared base, judged as vile by most of society. Well, Tenzin wouldn't be the first man who'd simply dismiss her as a whorehouse madam.

"Lily, are you all right?" Tenzin's voice was gentle, compassionate.

She looked up. The concern in his eyes belied any judgement he might be making on her. Was it possible he sensed her weakened state?

"Of course I am." She felt her cheeks burn a bit. "I'm sorry about what happened. I certainly didn't wish your introduction to my school to happen this way."

Tenzin was silent a moment. "That was not my introduction to your school. Your hospitality and generous release of my *yang* were my introductions. As far as what happened here, I understand the ways of men. He is obviously a cruel bully. I don't judge you for that."

His kind answer began to rebalance the upset of her *yin* that Tzan Ru had caused. Her breathing evened out and relaxation tingled in her hands.

"He used to beat Jade," she said. "When I found her, she was covered with bruises and cuts worse than you saw her now. She had nowhere else to go." No sooner was the admission out than she realised she'd trusted Tenzin enough to reveal this much.

"I understand."

His kind gaze continued to rest on her. Her *yin* continued to calm even as her stomach fluttered. "I must teach the morning class. I had intended for you to observe, but I don't expect that now."

His eyes widened with what appeared almost a stricken look. "Why not?" He bowed his head quickly, as if remembering propriety at the last second. "If I may ask."

She stared at his bowed head, at the soft dark bristle of his hair, just growing in. "Well, perhaps you do not wish to have a madam as your teacher." She had not meant to sound bitter but couldn't stop the resentment in her voice.

He raised his eyes to hers. "You provide a place for your students to harvest *yang* in a way that is inconspicuous. At the same time, they earn their keep. Is that correct?"

She started. Was it possible he truly understood? The threat of tears stung her eyes, but she fought it back and cleared her throat. "You're correct."

Tenzin bowed his head again. "I wish to observe the class. I would learn all you have to teach me."

Lily sighed inwardly. She could not tell him the relief it brought her not to have to manipulate him as she was forced to do with so many such as Tzan Ru.

"I also would help Fen Chow to watch this place at night until he is recovered."

Lily felt her cheeks burn. "Thank you, Tenzin. Your offer is most generous. Perhaps I will take you up on it."

Ming appeared from in a rear doorway, a damp cloth in one hand. "Mistress Lily, Fen Chow is cleaned up as best I could make him, but he is still under the effects of drink."

Lily pushed away from the wall. "Very well." Her strength mostly recovered now, she went to the doorway of the back room and sighed.

The brawny man was sprawled over a couch. Soft snores buzzed in the air. He would be quite a burden this morning, even for her. But when revived by a Tigress's mouth on his dragon, he would serve as an excellent example of how *yang* could be manipulated and produce healing.

"I'll carry him." Tenzin brushed gently past Lily and strode to the couch. He leant over and scooped Fen Chow up, slinging him over his shoulder as if he were a sack full of rags.

Lily stared. His action had already caused her *yin* to awaken and swirl in her womb. Her jade gate eased open just a bit and caused her *yin* rain to flow. Was the Tibetan trying to make her dependent on him?

"Very well. This way." She turned and led him out of the room and through the back entrance before she said anything to embarrass herself.

As they walked the short distance down the back street to the compound, Lily resisted the urge to look at the huge man dangling over Tenzin's shoulder. She'd probably end up scolding him. It was a horrible breach of responsibility that he'd passed out drunk, but if she didn't look on him in his expended state, she'd be able to forgive him.

A young man off the streets who'd given much of his *yang* to her Tigresses, Fen Chow guarded them from abusive drunkards for her in return for his meals, a couch to sleep on, and the services of her women. It hadn't been his fault he'd fallen in love with one of them, a bitter girl who hadn't lasted on the path. She'd disappeared only two days ago, breaking Fen Chow's heart.

Lily did, however, afford a glance at Tenzin's arm where he held the unconscious man suspended over one strong shoulder. Impressive how effortlessly Tenzin had swung the muscular man's weight up and now walked as if Fen Chow weighed no more than a market chicken.

Just that glance caused memories to resurge. Was it less than a half hour earlier Tenzin's sleekly muscled body crouched between her thighs, that those hands were splayed on her buttocks as he brought her to a higher realm of consciousness with mere strokes of his tongue on her *yin* pearl?

A cascade of *yin* surged through her. More potent images of Tenzin's body, of the feel of his smooth hardness in her mouth, the sweet tang of his dragon's tears on her tongue, roiled through her mind, causing her body to soften and moisten in its hidden places.

Lily took a deep breath and concentrated on walking without tripping. It wouldn't do to be unfocused for her beginner's class. Day students came from other brothels as well as from a few select, wealthy households where the women had been sworn to secrecy, to take lessons from the Tigress School. She couldn't let her students see that one particular male was affecting her so much as to break her concentration. What kind of example would she be setting?

Tenzin followed Lily into a small chamber.

"Set him here, Tenzin." Lily pointed to a divan in the centre. "And make sure he faces this screen."

He deposited the sleeping man as she instructed and stepped back, taking care not to trip on the cushions that littered the floor around the sofa. A strange feeling tickled his gut, and though he didn't dare ask Lily what she intended, he heard women shuffling into the larger room on the other side of the screen and guessed at what was about to happen.

"Come with me, Tenzin." Lily gestured, and he followed her into the main classroom.

Tenzin watched the students file in for Lily's class. His heartbeat sped up slightly at the increase of female energy in the room. In his entire existence, he'd never spent this much uninterrupted time in the company of women, not even during his years of frequenting the House of the Jade Flower. He still wasn't certain of the wisdom of so much intermingling, but he also wanted to be in Lily's company. No matter what.

There were thirteen women in all. Their age range was difficult to tell. Tenzin understood this was because of the exercises they did and the way they applied a man's seed to their skin. Some of the women were very pretty, others merely attractive. All of them, however, had a glow to their skin and luscious curves, from what he could make out through the blouses and trousers they wore. Some had bound feet while others did not.

"Good morning, ladies."

Lily's authoritative tone grabbed Tenzin's attention as it did the women who arranged themselves in neat rows, all facing Lily.

"This morning we'll have a special demonstration from one of the advanced students, Fei Liu, but first, as always, we'll begin with the willow sequence. As Tigresses, a shapely willow waist is one of your greatest tools of seduction."

Tenzin felt a smile tug at the corners of his mouth. Yes, Lily had the curvy, trim waist of which she spoke, but it hadn't been the only thing that had heated his blood for her. He watched her clasp her hands together, fingers pointed upward as if she were going to bow. In the next moment, all thirteen pairs of hands copied her movement.

Lily gazed out over the rows of students. "Ready, begin." She lifted her hands up above her head and began winding her arms in a sinuous pattern, to each side, in front of her and then down by her feet, body bent over.

Tenzin found his attention riveted on her slim, petite form. Lily appeared to writhe, yet in a graceful flow of movement that made her look like a beautiful plant swaying in the breeze. He wished her long hair were still loose and flowing about her body, but she'd taken a moment to pin it in a bun at the nape of her neck before her class.

A memory flashed through his mind of the way she'd kicked Jade's husband in the leg and then chopped at his side, so hard he'd been forced to release Jade. Lily's slender build was quite deceiving. There was plenty of strength and determination coiled within her, and the focused precision of her movements in that moment had showed much training, not only in her Tigress discipline but in some form of martial arts. He suspected that even without the physical strength of an immortal, such as he'd seen in his dream through the rapid healing of her skin, Lily's cunning, intelligence, and steely resolve would make her a formidable opponent for just about anyone.

The willow waist exercises led to another set of facial exercises, concentrated specifically on strengthening the lips, tongue, and jaw. A ripple of heat passed through Tenzin's groin. He well understood the goal of those exercises. The facial sequence led into more strengthening exercises for the arms and legs, and then Lily stopped, steepled her hands together again, and bowed to her students.

The women bowed to her in return, and a moment of quiet settled over the large, airy room.

Tenzin watched Lily raise her gaze to the rows of students and gesture behind her. "On the other side of this screen, Tigresses, you will observe a demonstration of the next phase of your learning. One of my advanced students will show you the precise and proper way to seduce a Green Dragon and to harvest his *yang*. Please approach the screen quietly and with respect."

Another jolt of heated energy struck Tenzin. He kept his eyes on Lily for her next instruction. She stood aside to allow her students access to the screen then inclined her head towards him with a brief nod.

His breath caught, and he walked over to her, making sure that his shoes barely made a sound on the stone floor. When he reached Lily's side, her unexpected touch on his arm sent tingling heat through him. Her eyes were large, and for the first time since he'd met her, he saw a concern in them he hadn't before.

"If you do not wish to observe this, Tenzin, you needn't," she said softly.

Honestly, he didn't care whether he watched this demonstration. He'd had the real treatment, and that was better than watching. But if it meant remaining at Lily's side, he would watch. He nodded. "I would like to stay here."

Her eyes brightened a bit, and the corners of her full lips turned up almost imperceptibly. "All right." She turned to the screen. "Fei Liu, you may begin."

# Chapter Nine

*To whiten the face, the man bestrides the White Tigress. The green-robed woman sits astride the Green Dragon.*
~Madame Lin from *The White Tigress Manual*

Tenzin swallowed past a sudden lump in his throat. He watched through the holes in the screen as Fei Liu emerged from an unseen entrance in the room. The young woman was dressed in a white silk *cheongsam* that hugged her curves the way Lily's dress had fit her. Every swell of flesh was perfectly, smoothly outlined. Fei Liu's legs, too, smooth and pale, flashed through the long slits in the sides of her dress. Her long hair was pulled back at the nape of her neck, and the sleek fall of it hung down her back, a glorious contrast of black on the white silk. The only difference in her image of beauty to Lily's was Fei Liu's gait, a halting shuffle caused by her tiny bound feet.

Fei Liu carried a bowl of steaming water in both hands. Carefully she lowered herself to her knees, set the bowl aside and laid a hand on Fen Chow's leg. Her painted fingers tightened around his knee, and Fen Chow's breathing shifted. He blinked his eyes and rubbed a fist across them.

When his gaze alighted on Fei Liu, the large man blinked again as if she were an apparition before him. He started, clearly disoriented, but Fei Liu rose higher on his knees, and a beautiful smile spread across her soft lips. Lifting her hands to her dress, she undid the first few closures, letting the silk fall to each side. Small, firm breasts exposed, she gently pushed him back on the cushions.

Fen Chow sank back, eyes wide on Fei Liu's bare breasts. One large hand went to his temple and rubbed, demonstrating that his head hurt from the afterbite of his drinking. Fei Liu leaned in to him and began undoing his trousers.

Tenzin heard a soft murmur in the air and realised after a moment that Fei Liu was speaking quietly to the dazed man. After a second, Fen Chow looked up, his gaze directed at the screen. Apparently, Fei Liu had explained what they were doing. Fen Chow's eyes were wide for a moment, but then he seemed to accept the situation and sank back again, allowing Fei Liu to lower his trousers to the floor.

Tenzin swallowed hard again. He would have already begun to get erect at this point, but Fen Chow's hung-over state obviously caused his cock to lie flaccid against one muscled thigh. Fei Liu passed a delicate hand over the soft member, and Tenzin's own *yang* energy rippled through his body in one wave after another, as if the young woman were caressing him instead. He became aware of Lily close beside him, observing her student with an even expression.

"Notice, ladies, that a Tigress is always gentle with a man, always passionate and giving. Every touch conveys to him that he is special, unique."

Fei Liu moved her caress to Fen Chow's bulging thighs. The large man released a soft groan, and Tenzin could see Fen Chow's member stir. Fen Chow lifted his head, his eyes riveted on the woman's long-nailed fingers trailing over his bare skin.

"This man was feeing unwell," Lily continued. "He's suffering depression and has had too much drink. He's not a bad man, but he is troubled, as we all are at times. A Tigress's touch will stir his *yang* force, the healing power he needs to overcome his ills."

At this, Fei Liu returned her caress to Fen Chow's cock. The plump head now stretched from its sheath, and the shaft emerged, thickening with each passing second. The large man's groans of pleasure matched his growing erection.

"Ladies, if you can master the techniques you are observing, then those of you who are married can achieve a harmonious state in your household, and those of you who have yet to marry will know how to please a husband and prepare his *yang* to provide you with healthy, beautiful sons."

The authority in Lily's voice made Tenzin glance at her. He wondered if the scene they watched was arousing her as it was him.

She glanced at him, and the glint in her eyes seemed to bid him to turn back to Fei Liu.

He bowed his head and peered again through the screen just as Fei Liu picked up Fen Chow's cock. Tenzin pulled in a small breath at the sight of the thick member in her delicate hand. She dipped a cloth in the bowl of water and sloshed it gently around his privates. Then she put the cloth aside, bent over him, and closed her soft, red lips around the head of his male stalk. Fen Chow groaned. His head fell back against the cushions, chest heaving.

Tenzin felt his own eyes widen, glued to the sight of Fei Liu's lips as they slid down the large man's erect shaft. He could hear the tiny sucking noise her lips made as she swallowed the man's cock to the small nest of dark hair around the base. Two fingers remained at his root, holding him in place as Fei Liu slid back up. Her tongue came out and flickered delicately around the mushroom-shaped cap, and then pushed into the tiny opening.

Fen Chow groaned, and his large hands tightened on the cushions of the seat.

"It is a privilege and a great pleasure to give yourself to a man in this way," Lily said softly. "You are not only helping him by livening his *yang* and discharging the excess that builds up and can make him ill, but you are also balancing your own *yin* with his life force. This produces harmony in both of you. Nothing will bring you closer to heaven than balancing the creative forces of the universe."

Fei Liu released Fen Chow's cock, keeping her index finger and thumb around the base. She lowered her face to his *yang* sac and laved it gently with her tongue. Her action incited more groans of pleasure from Fen Chow who had come completely to life now, seemed to Tenzin cleansed of the effects of liquor.

Tenzin's own cock ached and pulsed hard in his trousers. Although he'd had release twice only a short time earlier, this demonstration made him long to go back to Lily's bed and experience her mouth and hands again.

Fei Liu returned her mouth to Fen Chow's cock. She swallowed him up again to the root and sucked him in a faster rhythm than before. Her head bobbed madly, and Tenzin saw her fingers massage the base in a rhythm against her mouth.

Suddenly, Fen Chow's hips lifted off the cushions. His fingers tightened and released on the cushions, and he raised his head, watching Fei Liu catch his emission on her bare chest He let out one long, soft groan, and then his head sank back, his chest heaving, legs extended.

"There you see, ladies, what advanced work on this Tigress path can bring you." Lily turned fully to the group of women at the screen. She clasped her hands together and bowed to them. "This ends today's class. Thank you."

The women nodded, and a flurry of approving murmurs rippled through them. Bowing to her, they shuffled and walked in the direction of the front hall, leaving Lily and Tenzin. Tenzin's body still throbbed with hot need, but Lily didn't look inclined to satisfy him at the moment. Instead, she turned and walked to the end of the screen. She slipped around it, and Tenzin watched her approach Fei Liu and Fen Chow. Fei Liu, still kneeling on her cushion, had wiped herself off and was caressing one of Fen Chow's thighs.

"Very good, Fei Liu. I see your careful ministrations have revived him. If I may impose on you a moment longer, please fetch Jade."

Fei Liu covered her breasts, then rose from her knees and bowed. Her *cheongsam* obviously restricted her movements, but she shuffled from the room swiftly anyway. Fen Chow remained reclined, his chest still heaving, his expression glazed.

Lily approached the screen and looked at Tenzin. Their gazes locked through the carved holes. "Tenzin, do not think I'm being cruel. It is crucial for Fen Chow to understand the consequences of neglect. As long as he wishes to provide his services and to receive ours, he must remain vigilant. Our lives depend on each other's care."

The distress in her voice made him long to comfort her. The best he could do was nod. "Yes, Lily. I saw what happened to Jade, and I understand." He couldn't deny the relief in her expression. Was it possible his opinion mattered that much to her?

A noise at the door made him look up. Fei Liu had returned and stood aside, ushering Jade into the room.

"Kneel before him, Jade," Lily said.

Jade nodded and obediently sank to her knees on the cushion before Fen Chow.

Fen Chow looked up. His eyes widened again, this time, with a stricken look. Sweat beaded on his brow and upper lip. "Jade? What is this?"

"Her husband returned and beat her in Plum House while you slept off your drink," Lily said.

Fen Chow gasped. "Oh, no." He reached out and brushed a gentle fingertip across Jade's bruised cheek. To Tenzin's shock, Fen Chow began to sob. He slipped to his knees next to Jade and cradled her head in his hands. "I'm sorry," he whispered through his sobs. "I'm so sorry." He leaned over and pressed his forehead to Jade's, stroking her temples with his thumbs.

A tear rolled from Jade's eye. She reached out and bid Fen Chow to straighten. He allowed his large body to be moved by her hands. Jade embraced him and stroked the long thick braid that had swung over his shoulder when he slipped down.

Tenzin wanted to turn away, to give Jade and Fen Chow privacy, but was riveted to the display of forgiveness. He watched Jade straighten up and hold Fen Chow away. She then reached down, pulled his fallen trousers up over his hips and tied the drawstring.

A gentle hand on Tenzin's arm made him turn.

Lily. Her dark eyes appeared misty, yet her demeanour was still that of the Tigress in control. "Come," she said gently, "I have texts for you to study this afternoon, before you go to stand guard at Plum House."

# Chapter Ten

*Swallowing from above and quivering from below gathers the* qi.
*Continual refinement of these will harmonize the* qi.
~Madame Lin from The *White Tigress Manual*

*Tenzin, turn away any man who requires an invitation to enter.*

Tenzin stood in the doorway of Plum House that night, unable to ignore the ache he felt. Lily hadn't said the word out loud when she'd given him the instruction, but he'd known exactly what she'd meant.

No vampires allowed. Of course, he didn't need to wonder why. Any Tigress who knelt before one took her life in her hands.

And yet, Lily had not identified him as a vampire. He knew the answer to that one as well. His heart still beat in his chest. Blood ran through his veins, brimming with life force.

He'd met one other like himself in his travels, a man whose heart still beat and yet who craved blood. Like Tenzin, Neville, an Englishman travelling on the same barge in France, had found a way to survive without gratuitous feeding. He, too, subsisted on the newly dead who needed to be drained of blood or those who were dying in pain and for whom a feeding was a merciful, more pleasurable way to pass from one state to the next.

Tenzin sighed and stepped aside to permit a man to enter. He crossed the threshold with a mere nod of his head and was picked up immediately by Jade whose injuries were well covered by face paint and a smile. When they were gone, Tenzin returned his gaze to the dark street, lit by a few gas lamps and the lights glowing from other brothels lining the thoroughfare.

Since he'd begun his fervent search for a teacher, he hadn't thought his heart could feel a heavier weight. Now he knew it could be worse. Worse than suffering because of his desires was suffering with the knowledge that he was now deceiving his teacher. How swiftly and completely she'd become dear to him, and now he would probably lose her when he told her the truth.

Tenzin's ears pricked up at the sound of shoes moving in the dirt of the street. The odour of rust, undetectable by normal humans, assaulted his nostrils. His heartbeat rose.

Vampire.

He was handsome, dressed in a caftan of blue silk with a matching cap. A long, thick braid hung down his back. As soon as he approached, his eyes locked with Tenzin's. Like two dogs in an alleyway, they stared each other down.

The vampire's lips curled up in a falsely polite grin. A glint of recognition lit his almond-shaped eyes. He stared at Tenzin as if he knew him.

A shiver raced up Tenzin's back. He studied the vampire's face, trying to place him. Very likely he'd been in the gaming parlour the night before, but

Tenzin had only seen Lily. The rest of the faces had been a blur behind the screen of tobacco smoke.

"I have heard that a man will never have a bad time in Plum House," the vampire said.

Tenzin narrowed his eyes. "That is true, if one is a man." He folded his arms across his chest and took a step back as if to allow the vampire to cross the threshold.

A defiant look slipped across the vampire's face, quickly replaced by forced civility. He remained where he was. "I do not go anywhere I am not invited." He pulled a coin purse from the pocket of his caftan and jingled it in obvious temptation.

"If you need to be invited," he said, "then you are not welcome here. Be gone."

The vampire growled, and a flash of bloodlust lit his eyes.

Tenzin stared him down and felt his own pupils heat to a soft glow.

In the next moment, the vampire's eyes dimmed. Without another word, he turned and walked away.

\* \* \* \*

"I may have found her." Zao burned with jealousy, an emotion that plagued him even after Wei Yen had made him undead. The sight of her half-clad body at her dressing table, however, made him glad he'd done her bidding.

Wei Yen whipped around. She'd loosened her long hair for brushing but now pushed her servant away. The woman bowed and shuffled quickly out. Wei Yen's eyes were as wide as they were fierce. "Tell me."

He drew closer. His mistress's scent invaded him, and he felt only his desire to please her. "I did not see her, but I did see him." The Tibetan whose body she'd lusted for. To think, he was a vampire. Not the non-vampire immortal he and Wei Yen had thought. The glow in the Tibetan's eyes was the only indication of what he was. Small comfort Zao had knowing his mistress would not have been able to feed on him as she'd desired.

She narrowed her eyes. "Don't speak in riddles."

"The one she took in the game. He was guarding a brothel."

Wei Yen's hand came out and swatted his arm. "You idiot! Why didn't you stay there and watch for her?"

His face, and his hand itched to slap her across the face. He held back, as always. Wei Yen was much stronger than he, and hitting her would be the last thing he ever did. He bowed his head. "I was anxious to report to you."

Wei Yen raised a small fist. "You're not telling me all," she ground out. "I feel it."

He resisted the urge to step back. He had once been her best student but now had no desire to tangle with the Shaolin master. Her burning need for revenge made a tickle of frustrated anger curl in his gut. Vampire or not, he wished only to live in peace with the woman he worshipped. "He would not invite me in. Apparently, whatever place he was guarding does not permit vampires." Strange, considering the Tibetan himself was one of the undead.

Wei Yen clenched her teeth. "Go back now. See what you can learn by dawn."

His hands tightened into fists at his sides, more out of frustration than aggression. He rarely ever expressed his feelings to her. His desire to please her had been his only purpose. But this could only end badly. Even for a powerful creature like Wei Yen, facing Lily Tan, an immortal who'd been able to slay an even more powerful vampire, could mean the end of everything he held dear.

Before he knew what he was doing, he found himself on his knees. "Wei Yen, please. We can be happy together, you and I. Stop this desire for revenge. I implore you. Let it be."

Wei Yen scowled at him. She stared into his eyes.

Zao would not be intimidated.

She glowered, lips curled back.

He stared, unmoving.

She slapped him across the face. Hard.

His head snapped to the side. He brought himself to face her again and kept his body like a stone.

She slapped his other cheek. "If you won't do it, I'll find another lover who will. Don't toy with me, Zao."

He sighed. To his grief, Wei Yen would make good on her threat. No matter what he did, she took other lovers. She'd wanted the Tibetan on the platform that night, in spite of Zao's complete devotion.

"Fine." Slowly, he rose to his feet.

Her look softened, but the glitter of revenge remained. "That's more like it."

He went to his armoire and changed into coolie clothing so that he could spy on Plum House inconspicuously. He would have to keep his distance. No doubt the Tibetan had smelled him coming even though he hadn't seemed to recognise Zao from the gaming parlour.

Wei Yen was back at her dressing table, gazing at herself while her servant, who had returned, ran the comb through her waist-length hair. His mistress afforded him a mere glance.

He stopped by the door of her bedchamber. "I thought you should know one more thing."

She met his eyes in the looking glass. "What is it?"

"The Tibetan," he said, wanting to give her one small barb on his departure, "is a vampire."

\* \* \* \*

*Two strong hands caressed the swells of her hip in tender circles. The touch stirred her* yin *cave, made the rain of her essence begin to flow. Tenzin…*

Lily's head shot up. The erotic touch on her skin was gone. Tenzin wasn't there. She blinked and passed a hand over her forehead.

Papers. The dark wooden surface of her desk. She was in her chair. She'd fallen asleep again over her ledgers.

Trying to ignore the irrational disappointment she felt at Tenzin's absence, she looked around the room. This had been her father's office nearly two centuries ago. His own ledgers, the meticulous records he'd kept of his silk and opium exportations, still sat on a shelf in the corner. Even though she'd grown to hate her father, she couldn't bring herself to discard his books. As a girl, she'd spent many hours sneaking into this office and reading them. He'd resented having an abnormal daughter, one whose feet could not be bound, and so Lily had sought to win his love and respect by learning all she could of his business affairs.

It hadn't worked. He'd sold her to Xu Yu anyway.

Slowly she raised herself from her chair. As she turned to leave the room, Tenzin came to her mind again. A flush of pleasure spread through her. An ache tugged her somewhere in a place she couldn't identify. The sensation was sweet, yet at the same time, deeply disturbing. She'd barely known him a day, and he seemed to inspire feelings in her she thought she'd buried with her childhood.

He was so pleasing to look at, his face and body rugged yet refined. He used his hands and mouth tenderly and passionately on her body, and the expressions that passed through his eyes, those deep, fathomless eyes, were unlike any she'd ever seen. Something about the way he looked out at the world and...looked out at her...made her think he already understood the things she taught without realising it.

She'd never met a man like him, not even in Wong Fei Hung, the folk healer and teacher who'd helped her master Shaolin fighting techniques. She wanted to enjoy the tender sensations that passed through her when she pictured Tenzin's face and thought of his unique being. And yet, such feelings were below a Tigress. One who aspired to the heavens in spirit was supposed to leave earthly longings behind...

She sighed and extinguished the lantern on her desk. Perhaps fatigue was making her maudlin and prone to the desire for romantic entanglement. Perhaps a few hours' rest would refresh her and strengthen her resolve.

Locking the study door behind her, Lily made her way through the moonlit courtyard to her chambers. Dawn would be here in a few hours, and Tenzin would return to the compound.

Damn, she wished she weren't so looking forward to that moment.

\* \* \* \*

*Perhaps I was better off without a teacher.* Tenzin watched the first hint of dawn light the sky. The other brothels had quieted down, and only an occasional drunk straggler moved along the main street. Most of the gas lamps had been extinguished by coolies, and a hush had fallen over the quarter.

Yes, he'd suffered all those years — all those centuries — with his myriad desires, but having a teacher and then losing her seemed far worse than never having known her at all.

A soft presence came up behind him. Tenzin glanced down into Jade's large eyes.

She bowed her head. "It is almost light enough to return to the compound," she said softly.

He nodded. "Are there any men left here?"

"Only one. He will be leaving presently."

Tenzin's gut clenched. Each passing second brought him closer to telling Lily the truth. Closer to losing her forever. Though she was probably sleeping now, he would need to speak with her at first light.

In moments, the customer left with a bow.

"We're ready now."

Tenzin felt a soft tap at his elbow. The five women who'd harvested *yang* from their customers that night were assembled behind him. Feeling burdened with the weight of impending grief, he nodded and led them outside, back to the compound.

Once inside, Tenzin saw the women to their rooms then started for his sleeping quarters. He hadn't rested at all in an entire day, and even his vampiric system felt a bit run down.

Softly, he walked along the corridor that led to his small room, but he couldn't ignore the ache that made him want to go to Lily, even if just to be closer to her.

The courtyard was quiet. In a corner of the compound, Tenzin saw a servant walking down one corridor carrying a bucket of steaming water. Muffled voices emanated from distant rooms, the sounds of a household awakening and for the ladies of Plum House turning in.

He reached the doorway to Lily's rooms. His heart gave a pound against his chest, and he hovered near the doorway. It would be unheard of for him simply to enter her room uninvited. He couldn't let his overwhelming need to see her take over. He bowed his head and stood, eyes closed.

"Tenzin."

His head popped up.

"Oh, Tenzin." Lily's voice came from deep within.

Goose bumps erupted on his arms.

"Tenzin, please."

His blood went cold. Perhaps she was in pain. He pushed open the door, driven by pure instinct to answer a call for help.

Lily's sleeping chamber was dark and cool from the lingering night air. He froze in the doorway and looked towards her bed, where the sighs and murmurs came from.

"Lily," he whispered. He could just discern the outline of her form on the bed, amidst the scarlet riot of bed pillows and silk coverlets. As he drew closer, he saw her long ebony hair spilled across the pillow. Her head moved back and forth.

"Tenzin," she whispered.

Every muscle tense, he drew closer. His breath caught in his throat.

Naked. She was naked. Her body writhed softly in what appeared the throes of a dream. She whispered his name again.

Tenzin's blood began to heat. Immediate desire stirred in his groin and strengthened. His cock surged and tightened, growing harder as he watched the contours of the leaping tiger on her body ripple with the erotic movements of her hips. The tiger's belly, fully visible revealed her gleaming *yin* petals. Each thrust of Lily's hips released her musky female scent.

His mouth watered, and he stared, riveted, at Lily.

His inner voice surged. No! He shut his eyes and turned. It was wrong to stare at her that way while she slept. And yet...

He turned back towards the bed. She thrust her hips up and whispered his name. His cock pushed hard against his trousers now. His heartbeat increased with the knowledge she dreamt of him. As far as he knew, no woman had ever taken him so deeply into her consciousness as to continue to think of him in sleep.

That understanding alone drove him to take a step closer. And another step.

Before he could stop himself, he found himself at Lily's bedside. Her scent swirled in his head and caused blood to pound through every inch of his body. His fists curled with the tension of his inner battle, yet he was losing quickly and dropped to his knees, just to be closer...

Her warm body emitted its sweet aroma, mingled with the lingering trace of incense she always seemed to burn. He ached to taste her lips, her skin, her dark, taut nipples that jutted upward, so close to him all he had to do was lean over a tiny bit...

Hands grabbed him. Tenzin felt his body in a firm grip. He was sinking onto warm softness before he realised what had happened.

He yanked back. She pulled harder.

"Tenzin, please," she whispered.

He caught a flash of her dark eyes wide open, locked onto his. Desire surged like liquid fire through his loins. He pressed his lips onto hers and tasted her wildly. She answered with the hot lick of her tongue against his. Her hands slid from their grip on his arms around his back and down, over his buttocks.

He groaned. Lily's softness and the way she melted underneath him made him wild. She no longer seemed like the controlled teacher, the reserved Tigress who doled out pleasure, but a woman, a soft, yielding woman who was giving her body to him, sharing the sweetness of her gifts with him, and who wanted to be joined with him completely.

Without thinking, he reached down and pulled the tie of his trousers. Keeping his tongue entwined with

Lily's, he used one hand to yank down his trousers and tilted his hips forward, instinctively seeking the moist warmth of her cave with his cock. The head found Lily's slippery opening, and he pushed it in.

Lily moaned. She pulled her legs open wider and clutched his behind.

"Yes," she whispered. Her *yin* cave held him with a suction that ripped reason from him. She tightened and relaxed her lower muscles in a rhythm that invited him deeper, drove him to continue.

He pushed. Her sex was so wet, so deliciously open, the slick channel swallowed his aching stalk with mind-blowing ease. A hot slide of pleasure radiated from his shaft down his balls and through his whole body as he sheathed himself completely in her wet, slippery heat.

Joined. Their bodies were joined. The closest two bodies could be without becoming one body. She felt so hot, so right, so--

Lily stiffened underneath him. Her thighs tightened around his waist, and she squeezed hard on his hipbones, forcing his pelvis in the opposite direction. Her hands flew to his shoulders, and she pushed at him.

Lily's awareness slammed onto the sensation of fullness in her jade cave. *Holy gods!* Penetration. She had to get him off of her!

And yet, when she pushed her thighs into Tenzin's slim hips, her mind blurred. The tiniest movement sent a swirl of pleasure through her womb, and she experienced confusion, uncertainty in which direction to push him.

He stared down at her, lips parted. Sweat beaded on his brow, and his chest heaved.

He was *inside* her.

Another moment passed, and then her mind cleared. Penetration was forbidden to Tigresses for the act robbed them of life force. Yet even if that had not been a tenet, no man was to possess her body in the same way Xu Yu had, especially a man who would come upon her in her sleep this way.

She pulled back, a sharp movement that made his dragon slip out of her. Heat tingled through her cave. The strange absence irritated her. "What were you doing?"

Tenzin sat back. His flushed skin darkened yet more. He bowed his head. "I'm sorry, Lily. Please forgive me. I forgot myself."

She yanked the bedclothes up over her breasts and glared. She felt deeply exposed, as if her being were as naked to him as her body.

"I'm sorry, Lily," Tenzin said again, more softly than before. Sorrow laced his voice.

In the silence that followed, she tried to ignore the pulsing in her sex, as if her body still craved the fullness of his dragon inside her. Damn her *yin* for softening this way.

Throwing down the covers, she launched from the bed. "This isn't going to work." She snapped up her robe and threw it on. Wrapping it tightly around her front, she began to pace.

"What do you mean, Lily? What isn't going to work?"

The panic in his voice made her turn. Immediately she had to look away. Whether Tenzin had meant to look like a beaten puppy, she didn't know. She took a deep breath. "I was wrong to accept you as a student. You've taken advantage." An image from her dream resurged. Yes, in her sleep she'd been making passionate love with Tenzin, but to wake up and find him between her legs, like a thief...

Tenzin leapt off the bed and was on his knees at her feet. His upturned face was frantic. "No, Lily. I beg you. I can do better. Don't cast me out."

She turned away from him, afraid of the weakness in her. She knew he'd think she was turning her back on him, but she couldn't let him see her shame. "I'm sorry, but I must curtail our training. I told you yesterday that there is no penetration. And yet..."

He gasped. "No, Lily, please. I've been around the entire world. *You are* my teacher. I cannot excuse my behaviour. Please."

She closed her eyes, steeled herself to refuse him again. Never in her life had anyone, man or woman, begged her this way. She wanted to think him pathetic, without dignity, but the sincere desperation in his plea touched her. He was telling the truth. However, truth or not, she couldn't let herself...

"No. You will find another teacher." She stepped away. "You're a sincere student. Any teacher would be honoured to have you."

Silence answered her. The energy in the room shifted, grew still.

Lily's heart lurched. Slowly she turned.

Tenzin knelt on the floor, his face a mask of sorrow. One teardrop rolled down the smooth plane of his cheek and dropped off the edge of his jaw. Holding his trousers closed with one hand, he rose to his feet, head bowed. "If you wish in your heart for me to leave, I will," he said softly.

Lily stared at him. She parted her lips to say *yes*. What stopped her, she didn't know. Strange as it was considering his crime, she did not utter the word. She sighed and bowed her head. "I cannot work with you. If you wish to rut, you may go to Plum House. I will speak with Jade or one of the other--"

"No."

The steely tone in Tenzin's voice made her turn abruptly. Hurt radiated from his eyes, mingled with a touch of defiance that made her insides jump.

"You're my teacher, Lily. I want no other."

Lily clenched her jaw in spite of the tickle of pleasure his answer gave her. "I cannot be your teacher any longer." Turning, she paced to the window, listening for his retort.

Silence answered her.

When she turned back around, he was gone.

# Chapter Eleven

*The Tigress first learns from her mother how to survive. She then has*
*three paths in which to begin her hunt. No matter which path she walks,*
*the Green Dragon is her prey.*
*She gathers the essences of the Dragon and Tiger.*
~Madame Lin from *The White Tigress Manual*

Lily remained tucked away in her study the entire day. She managed to finish her monthly books, and then sat for a long time in meditation. She had Fei Liu take over the classes while she took time to collect herself and to reflect on what had happened.

Pacing the length of the ornate carpet on the study floor, she curled her hands into fists. To think that Tenzin had mounted her in her sleep, as if he'd known her dream and wished to take advantage. And yet, the stricken expression in his eyes when she'd pushed him away, the contrition in his entire demeanour, neither were characteristics of a man in the process of rape. Were they?

She shook her head as if to jar herself from the wisps of doubt that threatened her resolve. Men were capable of all sorts of things, no matter how decent they appeared. Tenzin was a man who'd suppressed his visceral needs for a long time. In spite of his recent release of excess *yang*, no doubt there was much more stored away that the Tigress practices hadn't yet tapped.

The only thing that wasn't Tenzin's fault was the fact that she'd been dreaming of him. Erotically. Passionately. Their naked bodies entwined. She'd wanted nothing more than the thrust of his dragon deep inside her and his lips on hers as their bodies moved against each other's in a sweet rhythm.

To her chagrin, the actual sensation of his thickness filling her sex had not been unpleasant in the least. But what the act represented…she could not get past that. At least—

A memory of Tenzin's grief-filled expression surfaced. She tried to shrug it away and could not. He'd seemed genuinely wounded by her suggestion to find release in Plum House. Her words to him echoed in her mind, making her cringe. She sighed, shoulders sagging. How was it she was breaking down, feeling sorry, for him?

She took a long sip of tea from the cup on her desk, then rang for the servant who'd brought it earlier. She couldn't work with Tenzin, but she could at least apologise for offending him. After all, she was a Tigress, and a Tigress was gracious no matter what offence had been given her.

Old Chan, another of her servants, entered the room and bowed.

"Please fetch my student, and tell him I wish to see him."

The elderly man bowed again and left. When he returned a seemingly long time later, Lily's stomach tightened to see he was alone.

The man bowed again. "I'm sorry, mistress. I cannot find him within the compound."

She furrowed her brow. "Is he at Plum House?"

The servant shook his head. "No one has seen him since midday."

* * * *

Tenzin wandered the streets of Shanghai. He didn't care where his feet took him, even though he could never escape his shame and horror.

"You, coolie, stay back."

Tenzin's head shot up. He stood facing a white soldier in Western uniform, rifle pointed towards him. "I'm sorry." Tenzin bowed his head. "I did not see where I was going." He lifted his gaze to the high wall behind the soldier.

"See here, this is the foreign concession. Enter only with permission."

Tenzin nodded and turned. He'd have to look where he was going next time. He followed the length of the wall, now in an unfamiliar portion of the city. The street around the foreign concession was freer of the usual foot traffic of the city.

Several streets away, he came to the more familiar hustle and bustle of a Chinese marketplace. Carts littered the sides of the street, and the centre of the thoroughfare teemed with men, women and children rushing along, some dragging carts, others leading livestock.

Aimlessly, Tenzin went along with the flow of traffic. The occasional scent of honey reached his nostrils from teahouses and vendors' carts along the way. Although the sweet nectar made his mouth water, he resisted purchasing some with the coins he had in his vest pocket. He didn't want any pleasure, not after what had happened with Lily.

A sudden noise, different from the swarm of the crowd, men shouting, children laughing, women calling out the wares on their carts, suddenly tickled his hearing. He froze in the middle of traffic which continued on around him, unimpeded.

His ears pricked up at the urgency of the sound, as well as at the lurch it made in his gut. The sound of a human in distress was one he'd heard millions of times in nearly a thousand years of existence. A strange chanting mingled with the thud of fists on flesh, a man's grunts of pain reverberated in Tenzin's ears. Somewhere nearby, a man was being killed.

Tenzin slipped away from the main thoroughfare, down an alleyway. In daylight he didn't dare glide along the rooftops. One witness would be all it took to endanger the *Coeurs Éternels*, the vampires of his breed who fed only to relieve the suffering of the one whose blood they drank, and even though Tenzin himself hadn't named it and didn't officially identify himself with the sect of which he was the originator, he was one of them and did his utmost to protect them.

The sound grew louder. Cooking smells, animals, and sweat permeated the air, but did not drown out the scent of the dying mortal. Grunts of pain reached his ears, mingled with the sounds of the beating. And something else…

"Death to the Western dogs." The voices chanted in unison. "Long live the White Lotus Fists!"

The chanting grew louder, clearer. He followed the sound, just around the corner, the grisly sight—

White robes fluttered around fists and legs that kicked and pounded a defenceless man. The attackers' chants rang through the air. "Death to the Western dogs. Long live the White Lotus Fists!"

Tenzin's hands tightened to fists and bloodlust heated his eyes. He glided over, burst through the white-clad men to the centre, and threw himself over the beaten man. Fists and feet continued to rain down, the chanting unhindered by his action. That is, until Tenzin looked up, eyes glowing with the heat of his righteous anger.

The eyes above him widened, and the attackers scattered. "A demon! A demon!"

Their footsteps receded. Quiet ensued. Quiet, and the overpowering scent of blood.

Tenzin rolled quickly off the victim and bent over him.

Bruises, cuts, and blood made the man's age impossible to tell. Tenzin could see only that he was a Chinese, dressed in an expensive Western-style suit. The man's hair was short, in the style of European men, lacking the long queue of hair. Tenzin lifted one of his hands to feel his pulse and found the nails perfectly manicured. Whoever this man was, he was obviously from a wealthy family. No common labourer with rough hands and clothing. A few feet away, flies buzzed around a puddle of vomit. The books strewn on the ground and the scuffmarks on the man's shoes showed that he'd been cornered and overpowered. The man moaned, and a trickle of blood ran from the corner of his mouth.

Tenzin pressed several fingertips onto his wrist. The victim's pulses were weak, ravaged by the beating he'd received. His organs had been horribly damaged and were quickly losing function. The man's eyelids fluttered, and Tenzin felt the shudder of the death rattle about to course through his body. If he didn't work quickly, the young man would die in pain and suffering.

"I'll help you," Tenzin said softly. He worked open the man's tie and collar. His fingers fumbled at first, unfamiliar with the workings of Western clothing. When he had it open, Tenzin gently opened the shirt, revealing a bloodstained, lacerated neck. Once again, Tenzin pressed his fingertips to the tiny weak pulse. Death was coming swiftly, and the scent of blood made Tenzin's fangs itch and extend. Without waiting another moment, he curled his lip back and sank his fangs into the supple skin.

The man's body jumped slightly then relaxed. Tenzin felt a shudder of pleasure pass through the dying mortal who moaned softly. One sigh followed the next, and Tenzin felt the man's life force drain gently as he suckled, even as sensual thoughts and emotions passed through his mind and heart.

The man's body relaxed visibly as the suffering and pain drained from his body, replaced by sweetness and hope. A whoosh of breath passed from between his lips, and he went limp.

Tenzin lifted his mouth from the curve of the dead man's neck. He licked the droplets of blood that clung to his lips and gazed down at the faint smile that now curved the man's lips. Bending over down again, Tenzin licked off the puncture wounds so that they'd seal over. When the body was found, it wouldn't be obvious that a vampire had drained his blood. No one would understand the principle of feeding on someone to ease his suffering as he made the transition from death to life.

Gently he manoeuvred the dead man to a sitting position against the wall and folded the youth's manicured hands onto his lap. In spite of the cuts and bruises, he didn't appear dead, but as if he were napping peacefully.

Tenzin sat back on his heels and pulled out his skull mantra beads. He chanted under his breath so that only the youth's spirit would hear as he ticked off the beads between rapidly moving fingers.

Many hours passed before Tenzin sensed the man's safe crossing. He tucked his beads back into his pocket. No one had come down this quiet alleyway in all this time, and Tenzin couldn't be certain when someone would find the man's body. However, he certainly couldn't carry him out onto the main thoroughfare without bringing undue attention to himself. Gently he closed up the man's shirt and collar as best he could and left him on the ground.

Tenzin grit his teeth. In all these centuries, he'd never grown accustomed to cruelty. How could these men have attacked a defenceless man? Tenzin knew who they were. Boxers. Rebels who hated Westerners and, hated worse, Chinese who took on Western ways. Sadly, there was nothing Tenzin could do about these zealots. He could not give retribution, and even if he could, he wouldn't even know where to find these men.

Night fell, and he continued his wanderings. He ached for Lily and with his grief over her refusal to work with him. For several more hours, he reflected, debated, warred in his very soul over whether to leave as she'd seemed to wish him to.

And yet, when he'd agreed to leave if that was what was in her heart, she hadn't answered in the affirmative. He'd sensed her hesitation and grasped onto that shard of hope.

Tenzin wandered until well after midnight. Finally, in the small hours of the night, he found his feet taking him in the direction of her compound. Once there, he'd sit in meditation until daylight and then see what came next.

* * * *

Zao's ears pricked up. The sound of footsteps echoed down the street to the side of Plum House. He caught his breath.

The Tibetan was here, walking towards the large front door of a house on a street that flanked the boulevard of brothels.

Prickles of excitement skittered along Zao's skin. The dreaded task of spying on these people for the last couple of nights would finally bear fruit.

The Tibetan was let in by a servant and disappeared inside the compound. Zao glided up to a nearby rooftop and hopped across the tiles until he got a vantage point into the courtyard. Lights burned from the various rooms that lined the inner courtyard. This was a wealthy place. The Tibetan crossed to the very back and disappeared into what looked like a small room.

Zao got as close as he could. He could not drop down into the property uninvited, as was an unfortunate condition of being undead, but he could watch.

A light went on in the small room, and he saw flashes of movement. The Tibetan appeared to be alone and didn't seem to detect Zao's presence. He climbed onto a small cot, folded his legs and sat up, hands together, eyes closed. Meditation.

Zao growled to himself. It looked like another long night of waiting. Zao continued to skim along the nearby rooftops. He found a spot near a chimney that allowed him to watch, unimpeded. A glance at the sky told him that dawn was coming very soon.

How long had passed he didn't know, until another door opened somewhere in the courtyard. He leant forward to get a closer look at her. In the dim light, he wasn't sure, but she certainly looked exactly like the woman Wei Yen hated and wanted to destroy. Lily Tan wore a silk nightdress, and the moonlight showed the outline of her lusciously curved body through the thin material. Zao's fangs itched at the sight of her. Even from here, her life force was strong, potent. The blood of non-vampire immortals was delicious beyond belief.

Lily Tan strode across the courtyard. She seemed to be headed in the direction of the Tibetan's room. However, the light had gone out in his room much earlier and was now dark. She stopped and stared at the room, as if she were trying to decide whether to go in.

Zao watched her turn back in the direction she'd come from. Creeping back to the spot he'd been sitting in, he considered his next move. Of course, he needed to find a way into the compound. Wei Yen wanted him to kill one of Lily's people. A simple enough task if he could get close. Without the Tibetan vampire around.

He rose and glided back down to the street to make his way back to Wei Yen. He would take one more day to formulate a plan. He had to be careful. The Tibetan vampire had already seen him at the door of Lily Tan's brothel. One false move and everything would be ruined. One thing, however, was for sure.

He *would* get in.

* * * *

*Lily tugged at her bonds. The ropes cut into her wrists and feet, but they were of a substance that overwhelmed her strength, rendered her helpless.*

*"Still fighting me, Lily?"*

*She looked up at Xu Yu. The vampire's eyes glowed like jade fires from bloodlust, and his curled back upper lip revealed his incisors.*

*"Leave me alone. Let me go." Her pleas came out in a breathy voice. The rope drained her strength, as Xu Yu would drain her blood and her life force. Her body was not like other humans. She was stronger, and even though Xu Yu drained most of her life blood nearly every day, it always regenerated, providing Xu Yu a fresh body of blood to drink*

*and rape the following night. The torture never ceased, and Lily wanted to die.*

*Or for Xu Yu to die.*

*He chuckled. "Come now, Lily. You enjoy it, I know you do." He reached out and shoved the hem of her thin nightdress to her waist.*

*She cringed. Her heart thundered and sweat poured over her skin. She struggled against her bonds, but they only dug into her until finally, her body sank uselessly into the soft bedding underneath her.*

*Xu Yu opened his caftan and slipped it off. He stood naked before her. Lantern light gleamed off his stocky body and straining cock.*

*She whimpered and turned her head to one side, eyes screwed shut. It was of no use, she could never shut out the weight of Xu Yu's body sinking on top of her, the slice of his fangs into the side of her neck, the hard shove of his angry dragon into her womb.*

*All she could do was make her mind blank, let her soul drift from her body to seek a safe place...*

Lily sat bolt upright. Sweat dampened her skin, so much that her nightdress and her bedclothes were drenched. Her chest heaved from panting, and she found her hands curled into tight fists. Every nerve in her body was taut, and several moments passed before she realised she'd been dreaming.

The soft whir of crickets replaced her whimpers. A cool night breeze soothed her skin. Outside, dawn was just beginning to lighten the sky.

Then she remembered.

Tenzin. She'd asked him to leave. Their practice had barely begun, and now it was finished. But instead of feeling relieved, she felt mournful, heavy, as if there were nothing to look forward to.

A loud *crack* cut through the still morning air. She gasped and threw back the covers. Jumping out of bed, she pulled her wrap tight against the cool air and peered through the carved window.

*Crack!*

She snapped her gaze in the direction of the kitchens. And caught her breath.

Tenzin. He stood in the courtyard, his shirtless back to her, as he placed a log on the chopping block and raised an axe. His muscles rippled with each movement. In a smooth arc, he brought the axe down. *Crack!* The log split perfectly.

She was unprepared for the surge of joy she felt. *He was here.*

How could this be? After what had happened?

And how was it that she could possibly be glad he'd stayed?

Just as quickly, guilt replaced her elation. She had no right to feel happy at the sight of him. In spite of his transgression, she'd turned him away when he'd begged her on his knees to be his teacher.

She turned back to the window, pulled by the desire to stare at his lean, strong, golden torso, at the strain of his buttocks against his trousers as he split logs, one after the other, and placed them in a pile against the wall for the cook.

A surge of temptation gripped her to go out there, to apologise, and bring him back. Her body warmed at the thought. Even though she couldn't allow herself the pleasure of his touch or kiss, the prospect of his presence in the room comforted her in a way she couldn't understand.

Then she thought again of what had happened, of the way he'd come upon her in her sleep and penetrated her. The very thing she'd forbidden him. Such a lack of control was *unacceptable*.

She forced herself to turn from the window just as the door opened. Fei Liu smiled at her and shuffled in. She set a tray with tea and breakfast on the table and bowed to Lily. "Good morning. Do you wish me to fetch your student?"

Lily stared at the woman. Of course, Fei Liu didn't know.

She cleared her throat. "No. Let him do whatever it is he's doing."

"Yes, Mistress Lily." Fei Liu bowed again and left.

Lily sat heavily in a chair. She poured a cup of tea and stared down into the steam curling from the dark, hot liquid. The colour reminded her briefly of the colour of Tenzin's eyes. She blinked and raked her nails through her hair. Somehow she knew it wouldn't matter whether he went away or not.

Part of him was already inside her.

That evening at sunset, Lily stared at Tenzin through her carved window. The broom he held made a quiet scraping sound across the stones of the courtyard. The sound carried across the still air. He wore his vest this evening, and she could clearly see the smooth rounded muscles of his arms flex and bunch with each stroke of the broom. His hair was a bit longer now, and its ebony softness beckoned to her hands.

The same pulsing she experienced every time she looked at him now sprang up between her thighs. She forced herself to turn away from the window and pulled her wrap tightly around her as she paced. *Why? Why did he stay here?* She'd insulted him the day before and avoided him ever since as if he carried a fatal disease. Yet he was here, as if he...belonged.

She threw on a blouse and pair of baggy trousers so that she would not appear seductive and rang for a servant to summon him. Now was the opportunity to apologise to him as she'd wished to yesterday.

Lily's stomach fluttered madly as she waited. The shutters had been half-closed against the afternoon sun, and the thin lattices cast a striped pattern across the furniture. She clutched the edge of the table to keep from pacing the small confines of the room.

"You wished to see me, Mistress Lily?"

She looked up. Tenzin stood in her doorway.

The title of respect he used somehow made her feel desolate again. She hadn't realised how much she'd liked his using simply her first name. She clenched her fists and forced herself to turn away. Just looking at him filled her with an emotion she didn't want to give reign to. "Come in."

As he padded silently across the reed mat, she sat in one of the chairs and folded her arms. When he was standing in front of her, she waited, silently counting to ten in her head. Finally, she cleared her throat softly. "Why are you still here?"

A moment passed. "You are my teacher, Mistress. There is no other for me."

She lifted her head and met his eyes, keeping her own gaze hard. That wasn't what she'd meant to say, but was what slipped out. Perhaps *she* was the one lacking in control and discipline. "I told you I can't be your teacher. We do not suit."

Pain flickered across Tenzin's face. Even so, his gaze didn't waver. The expression in his velvety dark eyes unnerved her, the placid neutral expression mixed with something else…an iron will. "Perhaps you don't understand what it means when a teacher and student find each other. It's a miracle. The most rare gem on this Earth."

"There are other teachers," she said before his words could wear her down. "Great masters who can help you discipline mind and body without the temptation."

She hated the way she was speaking to him, especially when nothing she said baited him, and he continued to answer her calmly, with that kindness in his tone.

"There is no other teacher for me but you."

"Ach!" She shot up from her chair and strode to the window. "Has anyone ever told you how maddeningly stubborn you are?"

To her surprise, he chuckled. "Yes. My teacher told me."

Lily balled her hands into fists, resisting the urge to smile. She forced her mouth to remain in a grim line, something she'd done often as a little girl. When she was angry, she would fight against the impulse to laugh or smile at anything her nursemaid said in an attempt to lighten her charge's mood. She sighed.

"As I said, Lily, if you truly, in your heart, wish me to leave, I will."

She drew in a deep breath. "I wish, truthfully, to apologise for something I said yesterday."

She felt his *yang* shift; like a cloud, it surrounded her.

"There is nothing for which to apologise, Mistress Lily."

"Just Lily, please. And yes, there is something. I shouldn't have suggested you go to Plum House. It was an insult, and I'm sorry."

He bowed his head. "If you feel that way, then you're forgiven."

As usual, his humility softened her *yin*. Turning slightly, she pretended to be in thought when really, she was furtively experiencing her gratitude for his quiet presence. "That's all I needed to say. Thank you."

He lifted his gaze to hers and nodded. "I need to fix a leak in the roof of the main hall now."

Lily turned to detain him, but he'd already gone. She swallowed the disappointment she felt. Even debating with him had made her feel alive in a way she hadn't for so long.

Perhaps she shouldn't be so glad he hadn't left.

But she was.

# Chapter Twelve

*The white must seek the green, when fusing the yellow is seen. The*
*Tigress must seek the Dragon, when uniting the illumination is seen.*
~Madame Lin from *The White Tigress Manual*

Tucked in the alleyway behind Plum House, Zao
opened the vial of chicken's blood he'd brought with
him and poured it on his silk caftan. There was no fear
of running into the Tibetan at the door, for several
nights of spying had proven a large mortal man
guarded the entryway instead.

Zao smeared more blood on his face, threw the vial
aside, and then mussed his hair, ripped his clothes.
With a knife, he lacerated his own skin, on his arms
and chest, anywhere that would make him a
convincing victim of either thugs or the indecent
White Lotus Sect, notorious for attacking anyone they
believed to be supportive of the foreign presence of
the white ghost people in China.

Making certain his cuts were deep enough not to
seal up too quickly, he staggered out into the main
thoroughfare, moaning and clutching his chest. He
made certain to fall into a heap just beyond the
doorway of Plum House.

Eyes closed, it was a mere few seconds before the
sounds of women's cries poured from the doorway
and surrounded him. He kept his eyes closed and
groaned, the sound of a man in intense pain.

"We have to bring him to the compound. My herbs are there to treat him," one woman said. "Fen Chow, carry him, please."

"Yes, Fei Liu." A pair of large hands hoisted Zao up.

"Careful, you'll hurt him worse. The poor man."

Zao felt himself being carried and played up the role of dying victim by groaning and letting his body go limp. Deep down, he felt an ache in a place he thought he no longer had and cursed his own weakness. As a mortal, he'd been a fighter, eager for glory and strength. Now his greed had come back to haunt him. Such deceit of these unsuspecting people was wrong, worse because of what he would do to them next. He had truly become a demon of the worst kind. And not because Wei Yen had made him one of the undead.

But because he would stop at nothing to please her.

\* \* \* \*

*They were grabbing her again. Her mother and auntie held her small body in tight grips. She writhed and screamed, desperate to get away from them. If they had their way with her feet, she'd be in pain, unable to walk properly for the rest of her life.*

*A hand pulled off one of her slippers and a knife sliced into her foot. Lily screamed and twisted. Another arm gripped her across her chest, holding her shoulder tight. Lily clamped down on that arm with her teeth.*

*Her auntie screamed and let her go. Lily twisted her legs from her mother's grip and fell to the floor. She scrambled to her feet and ran.*

*When she crossed the threshold, she found herself grown up. Still in her family home, she sprinted across the courtyard sobbing. A single door lay ahead of her. She burst through the door into a shadowy room. A sudden cloud of peace surrounded her.*

*Tenzin. He was there on the bed, his eyes closed. He wore only a golden robe, and his strong legs were folded in lotus posture. He opened his eyes and held his arms out to her.*

*She sprang forward and collapsed in his arms. He pulled her close, and she curled up as if she were still small and sobbed into his robe. He simply held her and let her cry.*

*When she finally looked up, he was gazing at her, a peaceful smile curving his full lips. Peace flooded her. Her heart felt so full in a way it never had before. Bursting with gratitude, she leant forward and pressed her lips to his.*

*Ohhh, his lips were so soft and his love for her came through in the gentle way he kissed her back…*

"Mmm." The gentle vibration of sound made her eyes flutter open. The sound that woke her had issued from her own throat. Something soft pressed to her lips. Gentle hands cradled her back.

What? Not again!

Terror seized her, and she scrambled back, feeling the soles of her feet hit something hard, then her bottom hit the stone floor. Pain flashed through her behind. She stared up, blinking.

"Lily, are you all right?" Tenzin's face hovered over her in the greyish light. He reached out a hand.

"You're in my room again." Something wet was on her cheek. She brushed the heel of her hand over her skin. She'd been crying.

"No. I wouldn't do that." His hand remained outstretched, but she stayed where she was and looked around. Moonlight filtered through the carved screen window, casting shadows on a small table with one chair and a narrow cot.

"You're in *my* room, Lily."

She blinked again. "How did I...?" Dream and reality felt blurred. Her stomach and head reeled.

Strong hands closed around her arms and lifted her. The softness of the bed met her bottom, and Tenzin lowered her gently down. "You were dreaming."

She looked at him. Tears clung to her eyelashes, and she blinked them away. The moisture made her remember her dream. "I—I'm sorry. I must have walked in my sleep."

"It's all right. Would you like a drink of water?"

She shook her head. It was wrong to be here in Tenzin's room. He could see she'd been crying. She'd walked in her sleep. So un-Tigress-like. Her cheeks burned with the humiliation. She wanted to get up and run out, back to her room.

So why did she remain seated, as if someone had bolted her to the bed?

Tenzin's quiet presence hovered near her. Not close enough to heat her personal space with his *yang*, but enough that she could hear his gentle breathing and sense his concern.

She released a long breath and let her shoulders sag. "I apologise."

"It's all right, Lily. Just rest."

The kindness in his tone almost brought forth fresh tears. She glanced at him then away. These were not the words of a man who would deliberately violate her.

She'd fallen asleep in her own bed and therefore had come here of her own volition. There was no doubt of that. For several days now, she'd seen Tenzin only out in the courtyard, doing chores. He hadn't been in her room since...

A strange shiver passed suddenly up her spine. She looked up. "Tenzin, that night when you...when we...please, tell me what happened."

He cleared his throat and looked away, averting Lily's gaze. He rose from the edge of the bed and paced to the window. The moonlight outlined his strong body, bare-chested with only a pair of baggy, drawstring trousers covering the lower half of his physique.

"When I returned from Plum House, I wanted so badly to see you. I stood outside your room." He half-turned, showing her his soft, concerned expression. "I heard you call out my name. I thought perhaps you were in distress. But when I found you, you were naked, in the throes of a dream." He looked down and sighed. "I should have left right then. I couldn't, Lily. You were so..." he swallowed, and she saw the muscles of his throat work, "...beautiful. I could only stand there and look at you. I knelt down at your bedside. You reached out and pulled me onto the bed."

A chill passed along Lily's arms and up her spine. She covered her face with one hand.

Suddenly, Tenzin was on his knees, his hands over her free hand. "Lily, I swear to you I was wrong. I should have left. Your eyes opened, and I thought you were awake. I should have known better." He bent over and pressed his forehead to her hand.

Lily peeked between her fingers at his bent head. She'd often sleepwalked from the youngest age, waking in the morning in the kitchen or somewhere in the courtyard, not knowing how she'd gotten there. Her mother had stories of coming to her room at night and having conversations with her that Lily had thought she'd dreamed. Oh dear.

Tenzin's breathing rasped harshly through the small quiet room. Here she'd accused him of violating her when she'd been the one who'd pulled him onto her while in the midst of an erotic dream about *him*. If there was fault in this situation, it certainly didn't lie with Tenzin.

Unthinking, she reached out and caressed his head. He didn't look up, but a surge of breath escaped him, and he leaned more firmly onto her hand. She continued to stroke his head. "Tenzin, I can never apologise enough to you for what I believed."

He looked up and she read the denial in his eyes, glistening with unshed tears. "I should have—"

"Don't say anything." Her voice had fallen to a near whisper. "I was wrong. Let me apologise." She reached out and cupped his cheek. The way his eyes shone onto her made her *yin* soften. A gentle sigh shuddered through her. One of her teachers had once told her that dreams were often the mind's way of telling the soul its forbidden wishes and desires. After two dreams that had thrown her into Tenzin's arms...and more...perhaps her mind was trying to tell her the same thing.

Perhaps her relationship with Tenzin wasn't merely about attaining the immortality of her soul that would match the immortality of her body. A flutter erupted in the pit of her stomach.

Tenzin's hand closed gently over hers. Almost imperceptibly, his thumb brushed over her skin. The whisper of touch sent a pleasant ripple through her. "Come sit on the bed," she said softly. "It's wrong for you always to kneel before me."

Wordlessly, Tenzin rose and settled down next to her. He sat closer, and she felt the low vibration of his *yang*. To her surprise, he reached up and touched her cheek. His fingers stroked her skin with a reverent hush.

She looked down, loving his touch but afraid to tell him so. "I thought you'd left the following morning. I sent for you, but you weren't to be found." She heard the tremor in her own voice.

His hand slipped from her cheek. "I wouldn't leave you. I was ashamed and distressed, so I went wandering through the city." He cleared his throat softly. "I came upon a young man. He was dying. I stayed with him to say prayers for his soul."

Lily stared at him. The moonlight cast his face in shadows, a striking contrast of sharp cheekbones, long brush-like lashes and soft lips. The sight made her *yin* soften again.

"Every night I have these nightmares," she whispered. "They torment me." Her heartbeat sped up. "With the exception of my dream about you. That was the first in so long that was pleasant. The other ones, though they haunt me."

"I know." He turned, causing the shadows to shift, and she sensed his hesitation, as if he were about to say something that would anger her. "I see your dreams, Lily."

Her face burned suddenly with her shame. "What do you see?" No one had ever been privy to her secret fears, not even Fei Liu, her dearest student.

"I'm sorry. I beg you, don't be angry. I don't do it on purpose. We're connected in our hearts." He said the last word more slowly, his eyes scanning hers as if for her reaction.

Lily covered her face with her hand. "I'm not angry. I'm…" *Relieved.* She was relieved. Tenzin, knew of her past and didn't judge her. She felt a hand pass gently over her hair. The gesture was so tender, so sweet, she uncovered her face and looked at him with a tiny smile.

"How did you escape *him*, Lily?" Tenzin's gentle voice cut through her shame as his fingers recommenced their strokes against her forehead. The compassion with which he asked the question made it impossible not to answer.

Just before she spoke, Tenzin touched her hand. As before, he held it gently and brushed his thumb back and forth across the soft flesh of her palm.

She pulled in a deep breath. Never had she spoken to another soul of her childhood, not even to Master Wong in the years she'd been his pupil. She'd trusted Master Wong with her life, but not with her soul.

Was this possible? Did she really trust Tenzin with her soul? With her heart? Perhaps she was simply desperate to unburden herself, to cleanse her spirit through admission. However, she couldn't ignore the reality that it was Tenzin who'd been fated to hear her story.

"My father sold me to Xu Yu because my feet could not be bound, as you saw in my dreams."

"Yes."

"My father said he would not allow a woman in his household to shame him so. Xu Yu was an older man with several wives. He was as physically big and powerful as he was financially. He was a buyer of my father's silks. Father was relieved that a man would take a woman whose feet were unbound and who did not care that she'd put a blot on her father's name." She squeezed her eyes shut against the pain, the agony of her father's hatred and shame.

Tenzin squeezed her hand. The tiny movement filled her with a sense of safety.

"My father kept me at home until I was twelve. That's when Xu Yu offered to buy me. For several years, Xu Yu didn't didn't touch me. But then, when I was fifteen he…raped me." She closed her eyes against the grief. In that moment, she couldn't consider going on. But then Tenzin laced his fingers with hers, and she felt bolstered. "He violated me every night."

"Lily." Tenzin's whisper was full of compassion. His fingertips squeezed her shoulder. It was as if he experienced her pain and shame with her. Could there really be a connection between the two of them as he claimed?

She took a shuddering breath. She'd gone this far and though the pain resurged, clawed at her heart, she felt a bit freer. "Xu Yu fed on me as well. He was a vampire." She opened her eyes to see Tenzin's reaction. He nodded, but his face was turned, shadowed, and she could not see his expression. His hand, however, remained gently entwined with hers. "He didn't suck enough of my blood to kill me or make me one of his kind, but enough to make me hate him."

"How did you get away from him?" Tenzin's voice was heavy, thick with an emotion that conveyed to her the heartache he felt from hearing her story.

"A servant in the house took pity on me. She was an older woman. She said she had seen so many helpless young victims of his. One day, after Xu Yu had just left me, she gave me a knife and told me what to do. She told me she'd once slain many vampires and described to me the exact spot on their bodies that would let them die if stabbed. When she prepared me for his visit the next night, she made my bonds looser so that I could pull them easily away and slay him as he fed on me." Lily winced at the image her words conjured.

"I ran away to the north, to Laoxin. A woman there took me in and taught me the way of the White Tigress. I had never heard of this path, but when she told me that it was a way to control sexuality, to control the life force of both myself and any man I came into contact with, I became her willing student. She told me I would never have to suffer a man's penetration again if I didn't wish it. I felt empowered, in control, and believed I would never have to fear again what had been done to me."

She glanced at Tenzin again. He'd tilted his face slightly more towards her, and she sensed that he listened with careful attention even though his eyes reflected deep sadness.

She looked down at their joined hands. The sight brought a sweet ache. "When my family died," she continued softly, "I returned here, to my home, and made it into this shelter for women. I vowed to continue the work of the White Tigress to help girls who had been harmed the way I had been at the hands of men."

She fell silent and took a deep breath. Although she felt cleansed, she tensed, waiting for Tenzin to slip his hand from hers and coil back in horror. A tiny corner of her mind knew this was irrational, yet she felt it just the same. When she dared a glance at his face, her mouth dropped slightly open.

A tear rolled down Tenzin's cheek. He lifted her hand to his lips and pressed them softly into her skin. His eyes closed, he nuzzled her hand with a tenderness that intensified the sweet ache.

Finally, he lowered their joined hands and gazed at her. The moonlight in the room had brightened, and Lily could see the track the teardrop had left on his smooth cheek.

"It's a wonder you don't hate men altogether," he said softly. "But I haven't seen you ill-treat any of the men you bring to this place. They are housed, fed, and clothed. They perform services for you, but are not forced into doing so, as far as I can discern."

"You are right. No man is forced into a sexual act. Their services are freely given. Some pay for a Tigress to pleasure them, a few wish for training as a Jade Dragon. Anyone in need is free to come and go as he or she wishes. This is a school, a safe haven, not a prison." Lily realised she had been gripping Tenzin's hand all this time. She loosened her hold. "I'm sorry."

"It's all right." He squeezed her hand again. "You were very brave. And you were right to slay this...vampire and escape." He brushed his thumb across her hand. "You've suffered a great deal."

She pushed out a hard breath as hot tears slipped from her eyes. Tenzin's hand caressed her back in warm circles, as if giving her permission to cry. Her heart lurched with a flood of memories. Tenzin's hand stilled on her back. Such kindness radiated through his touch.

Seeing his face infused her with more of that comfort. Perhaps she wouldn't have met Tenzin had she not returned to this place of pain. She'd taken a home of sadness and suffering and transformed it into a school where men and women could find harmony instead of more strife between them.

The heaviness lifted. Perhaps a gentle man like Tenzin was some sort of heavenly reward for the salvaging she'd done with her life or for, perhaps, having helped others in some way.

He gazed at her, and she sensed his energy shift. A tickle of waking *yin* moved in her stomach. The warmth expanded like a soft fan through her belly and into her breasts. A memory of Tenzin on top of her, between her thighs, his dragon buried inside her, surfaced. Her impulse was to push it away, but in the wake of the peace she felt, she let the image be, let her mind rest on the quality of it, the feel and smells, the warmth, the pleasure.

Truly, Tenzin's dragon filling her *yin* cave with his potent thickness had not been painful. Not in the least.

The only obstacle had been her fears, beliefs about penetration she carried from the past. But not all men were Xu Yu. In fact, very few were quite that brutal. Thank the gods for Fen Chow and Master Wong, men who'd shown her the possibilities. And then...Tenzin...

Indeed, the very dream that had caused her to reach for Tenzin in the first place had been delightfully erotic. There, she'd writhed and demanded his penetration, delighted in it. In her dream, neither she nor Tenzin had joined with any fears or beliefs about sin. There had been only pleasure, sweetness, and a union of their spirits with their bodies. She'd felt that he was her...

Oh! The dream! It had been *her* dream, yet when she'd accused Tenzin of raping her, he'd not denied it, instead insisting he was at fault. The question she'd forgotten to ask the entire conversation now surfaced. "Tenzin, I need to ask you something."

"Anything, Lily."

She raised her gaze to his. "When I first woke up and found you inside me, why did you not try to defend yourself?"

He bowed his head. "I felt so guilty for not having left your bedroom in the first place, I didn't think it mattered whether you'd pulled me onto you. I shouldn't have been there. Once I saw you weren't in pain, I should have turned and walked right out. Instead I stared at you. I came even closer."

His answer stirred her *yin*. He'd said before that her beauty kept him rooted, unable to turn away. Certainly men had said such things to women in the past to gain their favours, but Tenzin was so sincere, so kind, and he'd refused the favours of her other Tigresses, that it became effortless to believe her beauty was unique to him.

Warm energy tingled through her arm, travelling to the rest of her body. She felt safe and calm. "I don't wish to be hard and mistrusting, the way I have been with you these last couple of days. I'm sorry. I so much want to believe your kindness is real."

He looked at her, his handsome face outlined in the moonlight through the carvings in the window. "It's real, Lily. I promise you. And I do understand why you would mistrust, especially after everything you just told me."

She sighed. "Where? How? How did you learn to be so kind? Please tell me? I know so little about you."

Tenzin's cheeks burned and guilt washed over him. The tone of hopefulness in her voice served as a stark reminder of his violation of one of the great principles of his faith. He was concealing from her the fact that he was a vampire. He dreaded the moment when he would have to risk losing her when he told her the truth. And he would have to tell her the truth. He cleared his throat so that he could speak past the horrible choking lump that had formed. "I'm a simple man, Lily."

A tiny smile curved her lips. She reached up and touched his cheek. Tenzin's eyes fluttered closed at the sweet contact. Her touch conveyed much tenderness hidden within her, and he'd felt it when she'd caressed his head earlier.

"You don't seem simple at all, Tenzin. Not to me."

He bowed his head. "I grew up in the Himalayas. In Tibet, it's an honour to have a son in the family become a Buddhist monk. That seemed to be my path, at least during my youth. I lived as a monk in a monastery most of my life, in prayer and meditation, tucked away in the mountains far from worldly amusements and luxuries until..." He fell silent, and his gut churned with sudden violence. How could he tell her what he was after what had happened to her? He'd lose her for sure. "Until it was made clear to me that such a path wasn't my destiny." He brushed his thumb across the Lily's smooth skin.

"How was it made clear to you?"

He stared at her. How could he answer her honestly, that he had been fed upon and made into the same kind of creature that had enslaved her and violated her repeatedly?

Several moments passed before he could answer her. "My destiny was to come here. To be with you. Just to be near you. To learn from you..." The last was said in little more than a whisper.

Lily's breath caught softly, and Tenzin could sense all the thoughts and emotions churning inside her. He saw that she wanted to believe in him, desperately needed to believe. In spite of her inner strength and discipline, he sensed that she felt completeness in his presence, for her and for him. He too, felt that completeness, in a place so deep inside him no words could describe it.

"Tenzin, truthfully, you are as much or more of a teacher than I." She bowed her head to him.

His stomach wrenched. It was a monumental gesture for a woman like Lily to have bowed to him and made such an admission. If she only knew the truth.

He could feel her preparing for something. "Maybe I've been wrong," she said slowly. "Maybe if I...allowed you to – to..." Her hand trembled in his. She moistened her lips and began again. "Perhaps if you were to...enter me...as before..."

His heart lurched. Was she possibly asking what he thought? He started to protest, but stopped, seeing how much it cost her to say the words, and he waited patiently, knowing how important it was for her to utter them.

"Maybe it would cure the nightmares." Seconds of silence passed, and then she whispered, "I have believed myself to be in control all these years, yet, if I live in fear of penetration, then I am actually *being* controlled. Does that make sense?"

He nodded even though his gut churned. "Yes, that makes a great deal of sense. I have lived the same way, controlled by my hatred of my desires." He exhaled, resisting the urge to pull away. What would she do if she realised she was asking this of a *vampire*? Not only that, but one who had lied to her, had violated one of the main precepts of his faith?

Yet, his cock surged at the melting of her resistance. It was all he could do not to reach out and lay her back on the bed right this moment. What kind of monster was he, even *entertaining* the idea of making love to her now?

Her hand stroked his temple and came down to cup his cheek. "Tenzin, are you all right?" She smiled.

"You needn't worry that I'll get angry this time. I *want* it. So much." Her touch was tentative, gentle like the brush of a flower petal. He moved his face into her hand, to show her his gratitude.

"I was wrong to have stopped you." She moved closer, causing her warm breath to caress his skin. Her flowery scent made him dizzy, made his *likpa* ache. "I mean, perhaps destiny was trying to help me get past my fear." Her breath pulsed over his lips, teased his chin. The sound was heavier, full of growing desire. "You're the only man in the entire world I could ever allow."

His hand gripped the bedding. He didn't want her to see his inner battle. His mind swirled. The choice was maddening. Make love to her in deception or admit the truth and lose her…

She leaned even closer and pressed a soft kiss to his cheek, dangerously close to his lips. She pulled back a tiny bit and hovered, causing her breath to mingle with his in the small space between their lips. His body tightened more. He was losing.

Her fingertips whispered along his jaw. "Tenzin," she whispered.

Her female juices, her *yin*, were rising. He sensed it, smelled the musky tang in the air. Her body softened palpably, and her caress slid lower. Her fingernails grazed a light trail down the side of his throat then skimmed his collarbone.

"Tenzin," she whispered, "Make love to me. Please."

# Chapter Thirteen

*For the tigress to let out her roar, she must soar with the dragon. When the dragon's essence falls upon the tigress, it turns to jade. The tigress is then indestructible and can roam the Heavenly Abode at will.*
~Madame Lin from *The White Tigress Manual*

Without a word, he yielded. Whatever Lily wanted, he wanted to give her. He leant down and pressed his lips to hers. The kiss was as soft as a whisper, a gentle exchange of breath full of sweet beauty. She sighed and leant forward, into him, but Tenzin pulled back.

She looked at him questioningly. Her heartbeat sped up. Was he upset? He didn't seem to be judging by the way his amber eyes melted and simmered.

"Lily, you can stop anytime you wish. I would never force you. Ever."

He could not have said a more perfect thing. "I believe you." She inched closer. The sensation like a million butterflies' wings beat in her stomach.

He seemed to hesitate, to hang back, as if uncertain how to approach her. His careful way was so sweet it made her *yin* rise. The sensation like her body melting on the inside warmed her, sent pleasant tingles through her breasts and down into her jade cave.

"How did you...make love to the women you spoke of," she whispered, "in the House of the Jade Flower?"

His lips parted, and his eyes widened. His face was so readable in that moment she could practically hear his thoughts.

"I do want to know. Don't be ashamed." She moved closer, wanting his touch on her skin. Her breasts felt full, aching for his lips and tongue to release the *yin* tide that rose inside her. "Show me, Tenzin. Please." She reached out and skimmed the fingertips of one hand down the centre of his chest. Mmm, his smooth skin was warm, and the hard muscles quivered as her touch slid over them.

He groaned softly. A flash of movement, a gentle hold on her shoulders, and she felt his lips on hers again. One hand slid from her shoulder and cupped her cheek. The tip of his tongue coaxed her lips apart. His male scent filled her, and the warm heat of his body close to hers made her yin swirl.

For what felt like a long time, he kissed her, tasted every soft recess of her mouth while his thumb brushed across her cheek. Lily's Tigress instincts slid into place, her impulse to stay him with her hands on his arms, to pull back from the kiss, and begin the ritual of hunt, seduce, and bring his *yang* forth so that she could draw it out of him at the pace she deemed proper.

But the gentle swirl of his tongue against hers, the warm, slightly possessive pressure of his hand on her cheek, told her mind that this was different. In this moment, she was not a Tigress, and he was not her student. This was a man — Tenzin — touching her, kissing her, with his unique male desire to make her feel beautiful, wanted, safe, before he took her.

The way she had envisioned the sex act should be in her girlish fantasies.

Still, her *yin* pulsated, widening in hot circles within her chest, to the hardening tips of her breasts and down in her belly. Her lotus petals were swelling with want, her cave seeped with moisture simply because Tenzin was so close, simply because her body wanted his to crawl over her, his hands splayed on her back, and plunge deep inside.

Tenzin pulled his mouth from hers and continued the dance of his tongue over her heated throat. The delicate skin there tingled under his kiss, and she tilted her head back, eyes closed.

He paused over the side of her neck. His body tensed under her hands, and his breath pulsed hot. A soft groan vibrated against her skin followed by the flicker of his tongue.

The sensation made her melt. He seemed to favour that spot on her neck. Some hazy voice in her mind told her this was strange, but the force of her *yin* tide, now mingled with his *yang* force held her body in place, made her hands caress the bunching, shifting muscles of his back. The feel of them caused another surge of *yin*. Sheer womanly instinct made her fall back.

His mouth slipped from that spot on her neck. She pulled him with her as she lay back, and he shifted, slid upward so that his hips nestled between her spread thighs. He surged against her once, his delicious hardness muffled by the coverings of his trousers and the silk fall of her nightdress. For the first time in so long, Lily did not want any barriers between her cave and his dragon. Somehow, it seemed natural that Tenzin should join with her, bury himself deep inside her.

Her heart raced; her stomach fluttered madly. To her surprise, Tenzin rolled off her and lay down on his back. "You take control, Lily," he said softly. "Do whatever you wish. I'm at your command."

She sat up and gazed down at him. The moonlight had begun to fade and in the shadowy light of pre-dawn, Tenzin's dark eyes had a mystical sheen that conveyed wonder and desire. His lids were heavy, and his chest rose and fell with deep breaths.

Her heart raced now, and she felt as if she teetered on the edge of a stone cliff. If she let herself fall over, she couldn't know what would happen to her. The thought terrified and thrilled her at once. If she hung back and remained safe, the feel of the ground under her feet would be constant and familiar, but somehow the thought left her feeling empty.

Tenzin reached out and ran several fingertips down the length of her arm. The gesture did not seem to demand anything of her. He didn't tell her to hurry. He didn't say anything even though his *yang* surged and pulsed in the air, even though his dragon was full of life force, a bulge tenting the front of his trousers.

She glanced into his eyes, startled at the tenderness in them in the heat of his desire.

Gingerly, she fingered the drawstring of his trousers and pulled it. The flaps of material fell open, and the head of his dragon poked out. Now was the time she normally caressed the shaft and then went onto her knees to take it into her mouth and harvest the *yang*.

Not now. Not here.

Wordlessly, she started to tug down his trousers. He lifted his lower body and helped her slide them over his bottom and hips to his knees. His dragon sprang up, the thick shaft reaching upward, pulsing with life. She drew in her breath. Before long that thick member would fill her, the very thing she'd feared and dreaded for so long and yet now wanted, ached for.

He made no attempt to advance upon her. Instead, he lay quietly, gazing up at her. She knew the ways of a man well enough to understand how much control he must be exerting, especially a man who had denied his physical cravings for so long.

Emboldened by his gentle willingness, she stroked one strong thigh. She loved the feel of his smooth skin and hard muscle. She slid her fingertips down to his knee and up again several times before moving to his inner thigh. Finally she reached the apex and brushed across his firm *yang* sac. He parted his legs just enough to better accommodate her hand.

He groaned softly as she continued to knead his *yang* pearls. She expected him to reach for her, to pull her onto him at any moment, but he didn't. He continued to lie still, allowing her to do as she wished. His dragon jutted upward, harder than jade itself.

She leant over and took the plump head of Tenzin's dragon in her mouth. Tenzin sucked in a breath as, gradually, she took him in all the way to the short, dark hairs at the base. His delicious flavour filled her mouth, and the hard veined shaft twitched against her tongue as she slid her lips back to the head and then down again. He groaned and slipped one hand into her hair. His flavour, his hardness, and his appreciation weakened her body, made her *yin* juices begin to gather and seep from her core.

"Lily." His ragged whisper sounded agonised and yet still patient, accepting.

The way he said her name sent a possessive shiver through her. She let his dragon slip from her mouth and smiled at him. A wild pulsing sprang up deep in her sex, an ache she'd experienced so many times but had never felt safe enough to satisfy. Her inner sex quivered at the thought that soon Tenzin would fill her and expand her with his maleness.

She took hold of the hem of her nightgown, lifted it up and cast it aside. Tenzin's breath rasped heavily in the quiet chamber, and his chest heaved. She sensed his molten desire, how close he was to erupting. Most men of her experience would have already satisfied themselves.

But Tenzin was waiting for her. She sensed he wanted her to pleasure herself at his expense. He didn't want her to allow him entry until she had fully satisfied herself. She gazed at him in awe. No one had ever made her feel so wanted, so appreciated.

She lifted one leg and straddled him. Hovering above him on her knees, she lifted his erect dragon upward and lowered herself down. The plump head nudged her slick opening. She caught her breath. She moved her hips again, and her *yin* pearl grazed the length of his jade stalk. Pleasure flooded her womb, tingled like a spreading fire up her belly and into her breasts.

Tenzin's hands held her hips, and he groaned softly, yet he didn't pull her down, make her penetrate herself with him. He caressed her skin and watched her with large eyes.

She rubbed back and forth a bit more. Not to tease him, but out of the sheer pleasure of exploration, of feeling a man's loins against hers without the fear of violation.

"Lily." He whispered her name again.

The gentle wave of sound caressed her on the inside, tenderly reminded her of how much she wanted him deep inside her. She rose up and shifted until the head of his dragon pushed her slick opening. Then she lowered herself down just a tiny bit…

A tendril of fear curled through her chest. She reminded herself that she was truly in control. Tenzin would never hurt her. She felt certain of that. His hands pressed into her hips but there was not a hint of force, even though his *yang* must be causing pain by this time in his loins.

She lowered herself a bit more. Her moist cave swallowed up Tenzin's dragon past the head. She gazed down into his eyes. He watched her from under heavy lids. "Lily, you feel so good."

The raggedly whispered praise made her smile. She leant over and kissed Tenzin's lips. The movement caused her hips to shift down, and his dragon slid in farther. The thrust of hard heat in her cave made her gasp. Even though her inner channel was tight from years of Tigress exercises, the slickness of her *yin* and the swollen openness swallowed him up to the root.

He grasped her arms, and his eyes flew open. "Did I hurt you?"

She stared down at him. Pleasure tingled in her sex. She squeezed her lower muscles, and his breath caught. "Certainly not," she whispered.

Before he could answer, she rocked her hips. The way his eyes rolled back in his head and his grasp on her arms pleased her to no end. "Lily." Her name came out in a strangled whisper. His *yang* flooded him. The heated scent of his *yang* filled her nostrils. This force was rendering him immobile, unable to do anything but lay there, sheathed deeply inside her, accepting the massage of her inner walls on his shaft.

She began a rhythm, an even tempo, rising on her knees and shifting forward against his dragon. Each rock forward made his dragon lick at her most sensitive spots, places she'd long forgotten, even when she used her own fingers to stir her *yin*.

She moved a bit faster. Each rub of his shaft against her *yin* pearl heightened the blaze, the warm rumbling of enjoyment deep in her woman's cave. Her mind softened, quieted, and with her eyes closed, she saw only clouds.

She was floating, lost in the sheer pleasure of Tenzin's male scent, the hardness of his dragon inside her, his gentle caress on her hips. A warm flush of *yin* spread through her chest.

Another figured appeared in the clouds. A beautiful face with huge dark eyes.

Lily's breath caught. Kwan Yin, the goddess of compassion was looking at her. Lily felt tears rush to her eyes. "Am I in Heaven?" she asked the beautiful, peaceful face.

The goddess laughed softly. "You most certainly are. And so is he."

Lily turned and saw Tenzin. He stood next to her, smiling. Love filled his gaze. Peace and compassion radiated in golden rays all around her. Lily felt love from herself and for herself that she'd never experienced in her entire life.

She reached out towards Tenzin. His hand came up to link with hers —

*Yank!* Lily felt herself falling. The clouds vanished, replaced by blackness and the piercing sounds of a woman's screams.

Something hard and warm came up underneath her. She opened her eyes, blinked. The screams continued.

She sat up, feeling pressure between her thighs. Tenzin. She was hunched over him. Her legs straddled his hips, and a heated friction in her cave. He was still buried deep inside her.

His eyes too were wide, dazed. Then she remembered. Heaven. Kwan Yin. Tenzin had been there and had reached for Lily just when the screams began. He must have dropped from Heaven at the same moment she had.

Another scream ripped through the dawn. "Help!"

She recognised the terror-stricken voice. "Oh no! Fei Liu!" She vaulted off Tenzin, but he was as quick as she, rolling off the bed and reaching for his trousers even as she snatched up her nightgown.

Fei Liu's screams filled the air.

Lily ran towards the sound. Women poured from the various rooms, clutching their wraps. Fen Chow and several other women emerged from the main hall. Tenzin passed her, sprinting in the direction of Fei

Liu's quarters, and barged through the swinging doors of the chamber.

Lily ran in behind him. And froze.

A large figure hunched over Fei Liu, pinning her to her mattress. Her slim arms and legs flailed in her vain struggle to escape.

"Get off her!" Lily screamed and lunged, stopped by a firm hand. Tenzin.

The creature turned. Blood stained its face and vest. Its dark eyes, too, glowed with an unearthly light. Lily saw its gaze lock with Tenzin's.

In a flash, Tenzin glided across the room, grabbed hold of the creature, and hauled it so hard it sailed through the air and hit the wall. Plaster and wall hangings cascaded down with its fall.

The demon rose up and launched its large body at Tenzin. It ploughed into Tenzin, who grabbed the creature and rolled with it. Tenzin ended up on top, pinning the vampire, much larger than himself, to the ground. Lily stared. Tenzin's eyes glowed, and his lips were curled back, revealing a pair of sharp incisors. He looked up, eyes meeting with Lily's. "Stay back," he ordered.

For an instant, his expression became apologetic, but then the vampire underneath him struggled to free itself. Tenzin's pushed down on it. The muscles of his arms flexed with an iron strength that Lily had never guessed at. The demon cried out as if in pain and smoke curled from the points of contact of Tenzin's hands with its flesh.

Lily's mouth dropped open. She stared at Tenzin, at his glowing eyes and bared fangs. Was this the same gentle, humble man who had been making love with her moments before?

No. It couldn't be. Her mind reeled. The gentle monk who'd gone onto his knees before her was a…a…

Tenzin was a vampire.

# Chapter Fourteen

*The Dragon peeks into the Tigress's den.*
~Madame Lin from *The White Tigress Manual*

"Get out!" Tenzin said. His voice had taken on a deep, unearthly tone. Lily thought he'd spoken to her, but the eerie glow in his eyes was directed firmly towards the vampire underneath him.

The vampire grunted in obvious pain as smoke continued to curl from the skin Tenzin touched. Tenzin rose to his feet, dragging the vampire up with him. Something about Tenzin's grip seemed to drain the other's strength, and the creature backed up swiftly.

To Lily's shock, Tenzin released the vampire's arms. The creature bolted.

Lily followed it to make sure it didn't turn back around for Fei Liu, but the creature kept running, screaming all the while into the courtyard. It fell on its knees, flesh still smoking.

The contact of sunlight with its skin made a sound like oil sizzling in a wok. Mouth of fangs wide open, it wailed until there was nothing left of it but a pile of ashes and torn silks in the middle of the cobbled courtyard.

Lily stared at the wisps of smoke rising from the pile and swallowed past the dryness in her throat. Xu Yu had died much the same way under her slaying knife.

A whimper pulled Lily from her frozen stare. Fei Liu! She ran back to the room.

Tenzin knelt by the injured woman but Lily jostled him aside and leant over her. "Fei Liu!"

The poor woman was bloody. Puncture marks covered her throat. Her rasping breath was laboured, and her eyes were half-closed.

Hot tears rushed to Lily's eyes "Fei Liu, I'll help you." She looked over her shoulder. "Jade!"

Jade appeared in the doorway, face tearstained, bottom lip trembling violently. Behind Jade, Lily could hear the sniffles and whimpers of the other women. "Jade, bring my herbs and boil water. Now!"

"Yes, Mistress Lily." Jade disappeared, her sniffles echoing.

A soft touch on Lily's shoulder made her turn. She looked up to see Tenzin. His eyes still glowed. "Please, move away, Lily."

She glared at him, at the embers that were his eyes. "No," she said and turned back to Fei Liu. The Tigress's breath was rasping, and her eyes stared out, glassy, unseeing. Lily ripped a strip of cloth from her nightgown and pressed it to Fei Liu's wounds, hoping that the gentle pressure would be enough to stop the flow. "Fei Liu, fight, please." She gave the order though she knew it was in vain. Lily smelled death hovering around Fei Liu and could hear the woman's heartbeat in her own ears. The rhythm was slowing too rapidly.

She reached up to smooth back her favourite Tigress's mussed hair. Blood gushed from Fei Liu's puncture wounds, and Lily could see she was almost dead. Herbs wouldn't help, but she had to try.

Lily shrank down, over Fei Liu. Grief wrung her heart and mixed within that painful emotion was a stinging sense of betrayal. Tenzin had lied to her about what he was.

"Lily."

She turned and narrowed her eyes at him. "What?"

"I need to ensure that she's prepared for her next embodiment," he said softly. His voice, no longer gritty, resumed its smooth, kind tone. "Trust me, Lily. Please."

"Trust you?" Lily's heart pounded. The pain felt almost too much to bear, losing her beloved Fei Liu and the one man in the world she thought she could trust, all in the space of a few heartbeats.

Tenzin remained unmoving. The glow in his eyes, like jade fire, unnerved her. It made him seem so alien. "Lily, do you believe in your heart that I would hurt her?"

A groan of pain pulled her attention to the dying woman. Fei Liu's eyelids fluttered, and her heartbeat moved at a crawl. Lily's mind clouded. Allow Tenzin to touch her beloved student? After he'd concealed his identity from her? And yet...

Nothing made sense. The goddess of compassion Kwan Yin herself had smiled upon her union with Tenzin. He had been in Heaven beside her and had fallen at the same moment when Fei Liu screamed.

"What are you going to do?" she whispered. The sound was a labour to make past the painful lump in her throat.

Tenzin squeezed her shoulder gently. "I must make her dying moment peaceful." He gazed into her eyes another moment. "Please, Lily. I beseech you. If you don't move, I will need to thrall you. I don't want to do that, but I will if I must."

Her heart squeezed. Truthfully, Fei Liu could not be hurt more than she already was. "Tenzin, if you harm her further, I'll slay you." Her own words made her wince, but she felt cornered.

"If I harm her further," Tenzin said softly, "I'll want you to slay me."

Lily's mouth dropped open. Fei Liu groaned. The agony in the sound urged Lily to scoot aside so that Tenzin could crouch by her. Just then, Jade appeared in the doorway with jars of herbs. Lily waved her back. She watched Tenzin kneel down by Fei Liu and smooth a gentle hand over her brow. He murmured a chant of some sort, but Lily didn't recognise the language. Then he bent down and pressed his lips to Fei Liu's neck.

Lily caught her breath as Tenzin closed his lips over two of the punctures. She held one of Fei Liu's hands between both of hers and rose up slightly, ready to attack Tenzin at the slightest sign of cruelty.

Fei Liu released a sigh. The sound held such enjoyment in it that Lily stared. The dying woman's dark eyelashes fluttered. She giggled, then murmured, "Ohhh," like a woman in the throes of passion. Her hand trembled a moment between Lily's, and then went still again. Lifeless.

Lily kept hold of Fei Liu's hand. The woman had been her favourite, her loyal follower, and devotee of the Tigress path. Fei Liu's quiet presence had brought Lily great comfort. Lily's bottom lip trembled. An ache washed through her, and the world seemed the darkest it ever had.

Tenzin swiped his tongue over Fei Liu's wounds and sat up. Lily was horrified to see droplets of blood on his lips. He didn't appear to notice as he bowed his head and continued to chant, a rich sound that seemed to come from the deepest part of his soul.

She peered down at Fei Liu. The dead woman wore a peaceful expression. Her lips were curved upward in a tiny smile. Aside from the blood staining her blouse and skin, she looked at rest. Before Tenzin had touched her, Fei Liu had most definitely been suffering horribly.

Lily stole a look at Tenzin. All this time, she'd never once sensed that he could be a vampire. For a moment, she wondered if she'd just imagined the glow in his eyes and the way he'd frightened the murderous vampire by merely touching it. Maybe she'd imagined the way Tenzin had drunk Fei Liu's blood.

But no. When she glanced at him again, droplets of blood still clung to his full lips. His eyes were closed now, dark lashes resting on his high cheekbones. He'd pulled a string of beads from the pocket of his trousers and worked them, one by one, between the fingers of one hand.

In the growing daylight, Lily watched the beads rotate smoothly between Tenzin's fingertips, and noticed with a soft gasp that the beads were carved into the shape of tiny skulls. She looked back up at him. He seemed in a trancelike state, his whole consciousness focused on some sort of ritual over Fei Liu's body.

It made Lily feel like an intruder, as if her presence were a hindrance. Silently she rose and slipped out. Her tears continued unabated.

The other women were huddled together outside Fei Liu's chamber, clinging to Fen Chow. A surge of anger swept through her. A vampire could only have come into the compound with an invitation. Lily narrowed her eyes, needing desperately to blame someone for Fei Liu's death. "How did a vampire get in here? Which one of you let him in?"

Jade inched forth from the huddle of women around Fen Chow. She bowed her head. "Mistress, no one knew what he was. He fell down in front of Plum House, cut and bleeding, groaning in pain as a dying man. Fei Liu made Fen Chow carry him here so she could treat him with her herbs." With that, the Tigress began to sob.

Lily sighed, and her shoulders drooped as her anger drained rapidly. There was no one to blame. She glanced up at the now bright blue sky. The day was magnificent and yet, to her, appeared darker than hell itself. "All of you, put this house in order and prepare for Fei Liu's funeral. When you're finished, come to me." Best to keep them all busy until she figured out what to do. A bad feeling simmered deep in her bones.

"Yes, Mistress Lily," Jade said.

Lily turned and went to her study. She paced the carpet, keeping her body in motion while she focused her thoughts.

*The vampire.* He'd obviously feigned his injuries to gain access to the compound. But why? A vampire in need of blood could either seduce or accost an innocent and take what he or she needed. Why plot in such a way to gain a victim? And had the vampire needed to lacerate poor Fei Liu the way he had? To drain her so horribly she died? Lily's heart lurched in pain.

Yes, the vampire had intended to murder Fei Liu. Lily knew the ways of vampires, and if he'd intended to feed merely for pleasure or even to make Fei Liu into a vampire, the process was not so bloody and fatal.

That feeling of trouble in her bones intensified. For some reason, that vampire had targeted the compound. She pictured that moment, the nightmarish moment of running in and seeing it bent over Fei Liu's flailing body. It had turned, eyes glowing, chin dripping with blood.

Lily gasped. That face. She'd seen that vampire before. Her breathing tightened, and she clenched her fists as the memory resurfaced.

The gambling den! He'd been there, not on the stage, but with the woman vampire, the one who'd played against her for Tenzin.

Lily gasped again. She coughed as if an iron fist were closing off her air. Memories flooded in, memories she'd suppressed for so long. How could she not have recognised that woman's face? How could she not have remembered Xu Yu's daughter?

Wei Yen had been a girl then, but Lily had seen her so many times, the resemblance was unmistakable.

"No!" Lily hugged herself and bent over, panting.

Footsteps sounded outside on the stones. "Lily!"

Tenzin rushed to her side. "Lily, what is it?"

Lily stared at him. Her bottom lip trembled and the lump in her throat made speech nearly impossible for several seconds. "She—she's come for me."

Tenzin forgot the hesitancy with which he'd entered the courtyard in search of Lily. He'd wanted to tell of her Fei Liu's safe passing when he heard Lily's cry. Lily's face was paler than he'd ever seen it.

"Who, Lily? Who has come for you?" He searched Lily's face, seeing the shock and torment in her eyes.

"Wei Yen." Lily's voice was a near whisper.

Tenzin eased his grip on her shoulders. He reached out and smoothed back her hair. He could only pray that she forgave him his lie and trusted him now. To his grief, she pulled back.

"Wei Yen was Xu Yu's daughter." She glanced at the door.

Tenzin turned and saw several of Lily's students crowded in the doorway. Their expressions ranged from fear, to mistrust, to kindness.

"Leave us, please," he said.

They hung in the doorway as if uncertain as to whether to obey. Of course that was natural. Lily was their teacher, not he.

Lily nodded at them. "Please. I must speak to Tenzin alone."

"Yes, Mistress Lily." That from Jade, the one woman in the small crowd whose expression showed compassion towards him. Without another word, they moved away, and Tenzin heard their slippers shuffling on the stones.

He turned back to Lily. He didn't want to release her arms, but felt it inappropriate to keep touching her. With a brush of his fingertips he let her go. Thankfully, she stayed in the same spot.

"She's the vampire who played against me for you," Lily went on. "I didn't remember her. I did just now. She was a girl when her father enslaved me, but she looks so much like him. It must be her. She's exacting her revenge on me." Lily stood silently for a moment, and then her expression shifted, saddened. She swallowed hard, and Tenzin saw the delicate muscles of her throat working. He thought of Fei Liu.

"Poor Fei Liu," Lily said softly, as if reading his mind. He saw the struggle on her features. She took a deep breath, and an eerie calm settled over her delicate face. She looked up at Tenzin, and a flash of anger passed through the almond shapes of her eyes. "What of her passing? You said you were going to help her. How could that be? You're a vampire."

The way she said *vampire* made his muscles clench. He took a deep breath and bowed his head.

"I am an Eternal Heart," he said. "I don't understand how it is, but when my sire fed on me, my heart did not stop beating, and I remained physically a normal man except for my taste for blood and the fact that my body didn't age." He looked up at her and saw her staring at him, wide-eyed. "I, too, was fed upon against my will, Lily. I was in a cave, deep in meditation when a vampire came in. I didn't know what he was, but he frightened me. He put me in a thrall, rendered me helpless, and then fed until I was undead, like him."

He studied Lily's face for her reaction and swore he saw a touch of softening in her eyes. "Perhaps because of some good karma I earned, I did not become a bloodthirsty creature. I could never feed simply for pleasure or survival, but only to ease another's suffering. I've met another like myself, and he told me there were even more of us on this Earth. But I have avoided them and any other vampires, wishing only to find redemption..." he bowed his head again, "...which was the cause of my search for a teacher."

Lily didn't answer, and he peered up.

She turned her back and paced several steps. "Why did you lie?" The question did not sound angry. Lily's voice was thick with grief.

He watched her back and ached to take her in his arms, knowing that was probably the last thing in the world she would allow. "At first, I didn't think it mattered. The gambling den was full of kith and kin. It seemed that neither of us was an ordinary mortal. And then, when I came near you for the first time, I suspected from your scent, so sweet and potent, that you were an immortal woman. When I saw your dreams, the way your flesh healed when cut, I knew for certain."

She paused, as if she wanted to turn around and embrace him, then he felt her tense again. "Fair enough. But then after I told you what happened to me, about Xu Yu, what then?"

Lily expected Tenzin to fall at her feet, to beg and plead, and explain himself. To her surprise, he only bowed his head.

"I have no excuse, Lily. I can only say that I became terrified of losing you once I told you the truth. After learning of what you'd suffered, I was certain you'd turn me away." He paused, and she heard him breathe a deep sigh. "I've been on this Earth nearly a thousand years, searching and yearning and suffering. I'd finally found the one person with whom I felt some peace. I was wrong to conceal the truth from you. I'm sorry."

She sighed. As usual, his humble willingness to express remorse made her *yin* respond. She forced herself to think of Fei Liu, to let her grief squeeze out everything else. "So, is that what you did for Fei Liu? Eased her suffering by feeding on her?" She heard mild accusation in her tone but couldn't help herself. Even though she could not deny the smile on Fei Liu's lips or the way the dying woman had giggled rather than moaned in her death throes, Tenzin had lied.

"Yes, Lily." His eyes brightened. "Usually a soul takes many hours to transition, but Fei Liu took only moments. She was already happy because she'd been your pupil and had earned her Tigress tattoo."

Lily gasped. "She spoke to you?"

He nodded and bowed his head as if his admission would earn her anger. "She did. She said she'd experienced Heaven because of you and was ready to pass on."

The strength drained from Lily's body, and she sank to her knees. In a flash, Tenzin's hands were on her arms, and he knelt in front of her. Fresh tears slipped from her eyes.

Tenzin's arms closed around her. She felt their gentle strength and allowed herself to sag against him. She couldn't deny herself the comfort of having someone there, at her side, willing to help her and protect her this way.

"Fei Liu died because of me," she whispered. She couldn't speak at full voice from the thickness of tears. "It's my fault." Without thinking, she pulled back, grasped Tenzin's arms and squeezed hard. "Wei Yen is going to try and kill more of my Tigresses, Tenzin. I know it. Please, you must take them away from here. You and Fen Chow. Protect my women. She'll kill them all. I know her." Panic flooded, icy hot, through her body.

Tenzin looked at her, and his normally gentle features hardened. His eyes narrowed. "I can't leave you alone here. I won't."

Panic made cold prickles along her skin. A sudden wave of anger gripped her. "How dare you refuse! How dare you not help me, after the way you lied!"

His eyes pained, for a moment, then he squared his shoulders. "I won't leave you here to face a vampire alone."

Lily jerked back, out of Tenzin's hands. "I slew her *father*. No one was there to help me. Where were you? Not there, not in that bed with me when he raped me over and over! I am strong. Humans are not so strong. You know that." She took a deep breath. The even expression in his eyes, the stubborn set to his jaw was as maddening as it was oddly comforting. A man who stood by his truth no matter what was a man to be trusted. Even when he'd lied.

"I have money. Plenty of money," she went on. "Take them on a train to Foshan, to my teacher. Master Wong will take them in. I'll give you money, enough to keep them all fed, clothed, and sheltered so that Master Wong will not need to treat them as charity." She gave him a hard look. "Tenzin, promise me you'll do this. Promise me you'll take them to Master Wong."

He looked up at her. His dark gaze locked with hers, and Lily found herself trapped in the torrent of emotion she saw burning in his irises.

Just then a knock sounded on the door. It couldn't be a servant. The servants had all fled in fear. "Who is it?"

"Ye Cao."

"Come in."

The door opened, and Ye Cao, the woman who'd helped Jade after her beating, appeared, bearing a tray with a steaming pot. "Jade told me to make this for you. An infusion to calm you." She shuffled in and set it on the table.

"Thank you." The young woman poured the steaming tea into two small cups then set the pot down.

Lily could hear by the girl's breathing that she was horribly shaken and had been crying. She crossed over to her and placed a soft hand on her shoulder. Ye Cao looked up at her briefly. Her eyes showed gratitude at Lily's kind gesture.

"Listen, you must collect your belongings and prepare for a journey. Tenzin is going to take all of you to safety."

The girl's mouth flew open, and she looked, wide-eyed, at Tenzin. "But, mistress!" He's a—he's a—"

Lily waved a hand. "I will not debate, nor will I entertain any doubts or fears about one of my students. Go and tell the others what I said and collect everyone here in my study."

Ye Cao's lips worked as if she were about to voice an objection, but she bowed and retreated.

Lily turned immediately to Tenzin. "I'm sorry for Ye Cao. She's a foolish girl. Her response to you was below a Tigress."

He bowed his head. "I understand."

She sighed. Well, Ye Cao did not know that she and Tenzin had reached Heaven together. Ye Cao did not know of the heights of bliss Tenzin had brought Lily's body or the level of devotion he'd showed after only two days, supporting and encouraging her spiritual progress. Lily hitched a breath as the realisation hit her. With the exception of physical practices to contain his *yang* force, Tenzin had already fulfilled the role of Jade Dragon.

She glanced at Tenzin again, at the patient way he stood close to her. She did not expect the warm tingle of affection that flooded her in that moment. Heaving a deep breath, she looked away. Now was *not* the time for such fancies.

She resumed her pacing, walking fiercely as if she could outrun her grief. The very thing she'd worked so hard to prevent had happened. A vampire had violated the sanctity of her school and murdered her most beloved student. Her cubs relied on the Tigress school to protect them from the outside world, and now they were in the gravest danger ever. She didn't dare to imagine how much worse it could have been had Tenzin not rushed in and killed the creature.

Wait. Tenzin had *not* killed the creature. Not really. He'd simply touched him, and the vampire had run in fear, a fear great enough to drive him into the sunlight.

She turned to Tenzin. His eyes had returned to their normal velvety brown hue. The incisors she'd seen him bare at the murdering vampire had retracted, and he appeared as normal a man as she'd ever seen.

"Tenzin, why did that vampire run from you? Why did it go out into the sunlight to get away from you?"

He shook his head. "I don't know. My sire ran from me the same way, moments after he made me immortal. He tried to seduce me, but I didn't want to be with him. I did not want to follow his ways. I knew even then."

Lily stared at him. She didn't realise he took her silence for anger until he bowed his head.

"I'm sorry, Lily," he said quietly.

Again, his humility softened her. He must have sensed it for he lifted his gaze.

Before she knew what was happening, he closed a hand gently on her shoulder.

Her eyelids fluttered as the warmth of his touch invaded her, a pleasant wave that made her skin tingle. Unbidden, guilt stabbed her. "You knew I was an immortal. I kept my identity secret from you as well."

"Yes, but it didn't matter to me."

She opened her eyes and looked at him. "You don't care that I lied by omission?"

His dark eyes regarded her with a blend of sympathy and placid observance. "No. I don't care what you are. Or what I am. Not anymore."

His words made a shiver travel down her spine. "What are we, Tenzin?" she whispered, both scared and thrilled at what she'd hear.

Several moments passed with only the sound of the birds in the courtyard trees.

"We are... friends."

Lily stared at him as the word spiralled through her consciousness. *Friends*.

"Mistress Lily!" Jade's voice cut in before she could respond.

Lily turned to see the women crowding through the doorway.

Jade ran up to her. "We won't leave you!" The Tigress clutched at Lily's arm. The physical contact conveyed to Lily how panicked her student was. Behind Jade, the other women's cries filled the room. Seeming to abandon all propriety, they crowded around her.

Grief stabbed Lily's heart. She glanced at Tenzin, then at Fen Chow, who stood in the doorway, an expectant look on his face.

"Please, quiet!" Lily begged, a finger to her lips. When they'd quieted down, she touched Jade's cheek. "I love all of you, and it kills me to do this, but I couldn't live with myself if anything happened to you. You must stay with Tenzin and Fen Chow. Obey them."

"When will we see you again?" Ye Cao cried.

Lily sighed. They just didn't understand. But how could they possibly? "I don't know. Please, go. You must be on the train to Foshan well before sunset."

Fresh collective sobbing broke out among the Tigresses. Lily let them cry for a few minutes, then shushed them again. She looked at Tenzin with a *please help me* expression. He nodded and assisted her in herding the women back out into the courtyard. Lily followed, caught up in the crowd as they made their way into the main hall, to the front door. At the door, she stopped and turned.

"Please, hush. Remember all you've been taught. You're Tigresses. That's all that really matters. Now go, hurry, I beg you." She gestured to Fen Chow to open the large front door and embraced each woman as she passed through. All the women's eyes were red, and their cheeks stained with tears.

Tenzin came to stand before her. She looked up into his eyes. *Friends.* The word he'd used to describe their relationship echoed in her mind. She ached to believe he was her friend. In this situation, she was forced to trust him, no matter what he truly was. "Take good care of them," she said softly.

"I will." His look hardened slightly. "What will you do, Lily?"

She sighed. "I have a slaying knife. I will have to fight her."

Tenzin grasped her arm. He didn't need words, for the firm clutch of his fingers on her skin conveyed his distress. "I am angered that you won't let me stay with you. You're using my guilt against me. You realise that?"

She locked stares with him. Words froze on her lips.

His eyes simmered and glowed, not with bloodlust but with his obvious emotions. "Is this my punishment for having lied to you?"

Unbidden, images of him rose in her mind, memories of Tenzin touching her, kissing and caressing her. Never before had she experienced such heated depths in another being. No one had ever treated her with such care and appreciation. Now that was over. They'd been to Heaven together, and she might never see him again. The thought left her as desolate as had Fei Liu's death.

*We're friends, Lily.*

She resisted the overwhelming need to throw her arms around him. "No, Tenzin. I don't wish to punish you. It's—it's—"

"It's what?"

She blinked back tears. "You're the only person in the world I can trust with my precious Tigresses."

His eyes softened. Emotions shifted like a kaleidoscope through the rich amber colour of his irises "I will keep them safe, Lily. I promise." He leant down and kissed her lips.

His tenderness almost undid her. Against her will, Lily closed her eyes and let her mouth linger against his.

Slowly, he lifted away from her. One last silent look, then he went through the gate.

# Chapter Fifteen

*The Tigress crouches low beneath the dragon, then leaps to seize the Jade Essence.*
~Madame Lin from *The White Tigress Manual*

Tenzin watched Lily disappear behind the heavy door. He suppressed an impulse to run back, to pound on the door and demand that she let him in, but the sounds of female sniffles behind him made him turn.

He'd made a promise.

Looking out at the group of tearstained faces, he gestured. "We must go now. The nearest train station is at least a fifteen minute's walk from here." He passed to the front of the group and started walking.

A small hand on his arm stopped him. He turned and found himself looking down into Jade's large eyes.

She pulled her hand away as if she'd committed a crime and bowed her head. "Tenzin, please, don't make us leave. Lily is everything to us. She saved us. I can't abandon her."

Her strength and loyalty was admirable, but... "I promised Lily I'd take you to safety. I'm sorry."

He took a step, but Jade blocked his way. "Please. Let us hide in Plum House. We'll keep it locked up and dark. No one need know we're there. You promised her to keep us safe. I heard you. That isn't breaking your promise. If she needs us, we'll be close by."

Tenzin clenched his jaw. "I don't know."

"Please."

He looked down at his feet, at his dusty black canvas shoes against the dirt. Truthfully, he was determined to bring the women to Foshan because he didn't want to risk angering Lily. But...well...Jade was right.

Back in her bedchamber, Lily closed the door and sighed. She filled a bowl of water and washed her face. Then she pinned up her hair, bound her breasts and changed into a blouse and trousers. One could not fight effectively in a nightgown.

Once dressed, she retrieved her slaying knife from its hiding place under her bed. For a moment, she gazed down at the ornately carved handle and sleek blade, remembering. The knife she'd been given to kill Xu Yu had remained in the vampire's body. She'd not had time to pull it out in her flight, hearing the running steps of the servants in the courtyard. Shortly after leaving his household, she'd obtained a new knife from an immortal craftsman. This knife had protected her well.

Tucking the knife into her sash, she went back to sit with Fei Liu's body and to wait for Wei Yen.

Hot tears crowded Lily's eyes as she knelt by Fei Liu. Someone—probably Tenzin—had cleaned the blood off her Tigress's face and neck and had removed her torn clothing, replacing it with a white sheet.

Quietly, she sat, head bowed. "I'm sorry," she whispered to Fei Liu. "I failed you horribly."

Reaching out, Lily put her hand over one of Fei Liu's. The woman's skin was already much cooler. Lily closed her eyes as her tears slipped down her cheeks. Unbidden, images of the hellish scene replayed in her mind. Over and over again, Lily saw the vampire look up, eyes glowing, lips and chin dripping with her Tigress's blood.

She squeezed her eyes shut against the onslaught of images. Truthfully, the only thing that brought her any comfort at all was the faint smile still on Fei Liu's lips and the knowledge that Tenzin had brought Fei Liu pleasure and sweetness as she passed into death.

Lily caressed the dead woman's delicate hand. Fei Liu had been born into a wealthy family, one that had disowned her because her husband complained that Fei Liu did not please him. Fei Liu had heard about Lily's school through the servant's gossip mill. Apparently, Wife Number Three of Fei Liu's household had been in one of Lily's classes and spoken about it to a friend when she thought no one was listening.

Either way, Fei Liu had shown up on Lily's doorstep, alone and penniless. Within weeks, she'd shown promise on the path and devoted herself, body and soul. Fei Liu had been the first and only student so far to earn her Tigress's tattoo because she'd proven able to meditate her way into ecstasy without a partner's stimulation.

Lily bowed her head and whispered prayers. She realised the soft chanting she uttered was more for her own comfort than Fei Liu's, not only because Fei Liu's spirit had passed on according to Tenzin, but because the stillness of his presence lingered. The gentle energy generated by his devotions resounded softly in the air. Fei Liu had been well tended to in her last moments and afterward.

A cascade of warm tingling *qi* swirled in Lily's chest. The energy travelled up the back of her neck and continued its whirling to the very top of her head. Peace flooded her. She took a deep breath and replaced Fei Liu's hand onto the bed. She looked into Fei Liu's still face. In that moment, any lingering hurt from Tenzin's lie vanished —

"Lily Tan!"

Lily sat bolt upright.

"Lily Tan, show yourself!"

*Wei Yen.*

Lily closed her grip tighter on the handle of her slayer's knife and rose slowly to her feet. She retreated from Fei Liu's bed chamber and followed the sound of Wei Yen's voice to the courtyard.

"There you are, you murderous bitch."

Lily looked up, to a nearby rooftop. The lantern she'd lit earlier glowed, reflecting the form of Wei Yen, dressed all in black like a stealth fighter, against the sky.

Wei Yen's eyes glowed with her lust for Lily's neck. "I'm certain Zao took great pleasure in killing your precious Tigress."

Lily stared at Wei Yen and gritted her teeth. She refused to give Wei Yen the satisfaction. "Your Zao is a pile of dust now," she said softly and indicated the small heap of remains in the centre of the courtyard.

Wei Yen didn't answer immediately, but her unspoken rage filled the air. "You always were a murderous bitch. You deserved every moment of torture you ever received."

Lily braced herself against the vampire's barbs. "I didn't kill your lover. He ran into the sunlight. Perhaps his guilt for what he'd done to an innocent girl."

"Liar!" The glow of bloodlust in Wei Yen's eyes intensified. "I see it in your greedy, filthy eyes. You killed him, like you killed my father."

Lily tightened her grip on her slaying knife, the only defence she really had against Wei Yen. "I would never have killed Xu Yu, but he raped me every night and drank my blood until I was near death. You would have done the same in my position."

"He was my father, you fucking bitch!" Wei Yen crouched down as if she would jump down into the courtyard.

Cold fear prickled through Lily's body but then she remembered — she hadn't yet invited Wei Yen into her home. For a fleeting second, she wished more than anything that Tenzin were here to step between her and Wei Yen. No doubt he would have.

Lily saw Wei Yen's gaze fall on the knife in her hand. The vampiress let out a shrieking guffaw that spiralled out into the silent night air. No doubt, the sound was a ploy to frighten her, to humiliate and intimidate her and wear down her resolve to defend herself.

Wei Yen's eyes sparkled with a malevolent light. "Where's the Tibetan? I might consider leaving you and the rest of yours alone for a trade."

"I sent him away. You'll never get your filthy hands on him." What she'd said was true. She'd never let Wei Yen near him.

For a moment, Wei Yen's eyes widened, then she cackled again. "Ha! Lying bitch! I'm certain he left on his own. You'd never be enough to satisfy any man. My father felt that way about you."

Pain shot through Lily's heart. She nearly staggered at the cruel tone in Wei Yen's voice. Her hand tightened around her knife.

"Your precious man meat couldn't have protected you from me anyway." Wei Yen shook a fist at her. "I was going to go ahead and torture you, kill everyone you love, and leave you alone. But I'd rather just kill you myself."

Lily's heart lurched. She held her breath and stared at the murderous expression in the vampire's eyes. She would have to invite Wei Yen to fight her, otherwise the vampire would terrorise her and kill everyone she loved. There would be nowhere to hide. Nowhere on this Earth.

For a brief moment, Lily almost succumbed to the prospect of death. The temptation to die was nearly overwhelming. In mere moments, Wei Yen could overpower Lily, drain her of her life's blood, and then plunge the knife into one of Lily's vital organs, so deep that she would definitely die. Even immortals could be killed if stabbed in just the right spot. Centuries of suffering punctuated only by a moment of pleasure and affection here and there had been Lily's lot for nearly two hundred years. She'd loved Fei Liu and that little bit of sweetness, too, had been ripped from her. Any mortal she dared to bring into her heart she would also have to watch die.

Except for Tenzin. And even he could be killed somehow.

Lily slid one slippered foot forward. The movement was tiny, a mere fraction of an inch. All she had to do was let her slayer's knife fall from her hand, say a few words to provoke Wei Yen — Lily knew exactly the words that would send Wei Yen sailing down from the roof to kill her — and offer herself to death.

Something held her back. Or...someone. Her heart sped up. There was one being on this whole Earth who would be heartbroken if she died.

Tenzin.

Lily couldn't let that happen. She couldn't let any more of the people she loved be in danger of Wei Yen's wrath.

In that moment, Lily realised she had something to live for. Something *important.*

She took a deep breath. Inwardly she prepared herself to fight. She took one step towards her opponent and sank into an on-guard stance.

Locking gazes with Wei Yen, Lily raised the hand with the knife. "All right, Wei Yen. Go ahead and try."

Wei Yen's eyes went wide. She shrieked, glided off the rooftop, and charged. Lily dipped back, avoided Wei Yen's impact, and whirled around. A foot in Wei Yen's back sent the vampiress careening into the far wall.

Wei Yen shrieked again and bounced back. She landed on her feet, straightened, then whirled around and charged again.

Lily jumped high and flipped, causing Wei Yen to sail past her. She landed, spun around, and lunged at Wei Yen with the knife. But the vampiress was too fast. She kicked Lily's wrist so hard her hand flew open, and the knife sailed across the room, clattering to the stones.

Wei Yen bared her fangs and hissed. Her eyes glowed with bloodlust. She barely gave Lily a moment to regroup before she lunged.

The vampiress chopped. Lily blocked and punched. Wei Yen twisted away and kicked, her advances blocked and returned at each pass. One good kick sent Wei Yen crashing against the stone wall of the courtyard.

Wei Yen bounced off the crumbling stones and caught her footing. She shook herself, causing debris to slide off her black outfit. In the next moment, she raised her bloodthirsty glare to Lily. "Just for the challenge, I'll let you get your knife, bitch," she ground out.

Before Lily could answer, Wei Yen cackled and glided up onto the roof.

Lily waited in an on-guard stance until it seemed Wei Yen would truly let her go for her knife. With a running start, she did several flips across the courtyard, snatched up her knife then straightened, pushing back her loosened hair as she searched the rooftops. Sweat poured down her skin, and she panted, every muscle tensed and ready, rotating in the centre of the courtyard in search of Wei Yen.

A whoosh sounded behind her. Lily whirled just in time to avoid a deadly attack. Wei Yen grunted and sailed at her. One sharp kick to her hand caused the knife to clatter again to the stones. When Wei Yen glided back out of reach, Lily took a running jump. She sailed through the air, defying gravity, and delivered a battery of kicks, the famous, deadly No Shadow Kick that Master Wong had taught Lily.

Wei Yen flew, helpless under the assault, towards the sleeping quarters.

The vampiress landed on her feet, but Lily lunged and battered her in the opposite direction with another No Shadow Kick. Wei Yen staggered back, almost crashing into the doorways of the main hall. Lily used that split second to lunge for her knife, but Wei Yen was behind her and grabbed her ankle.

Lily crashed to the ground. She cried out in pain as something sharp pierced the skin of her calf. Whatever it was tore right through her trousers. Lily looked over her shoulder and saw Wei Yen bent over her leg, fangs sunk into her skin.

Ahhh, the agony! Pain shuddered through her calf around the vampiress's fangs. Lily tried to shake Wei Yen off of her, but Wei Yen only bit her more deeply. Planting her hands on the ground, Lily used all her strength to inch forward. Pain sliced through her leg as she dragged herself and Wei Yen inches across the floor.

Wei Yen raked sharp nails across the back of Lily's thigh and then on her lower back. Lily grunted again and reached for her knife. Another…inch…and…

Her hand closed around the handle. She pulled in a quick, deep breath and gathered her strength. She took one second to mark the spot with her gaze then, in one swift motion, sat up, raised the knife, and plunged it into Wei Yen's back, right where her heart was...

"Ahhhh!" Wei Yen's shriek cut the night. Its echoes spiralled off the rooftops.

Wei Yen released Lily's leg, and Lily rose up, pushed the knife in deeper and held it down. Wei Yen struggled, pulled her body away, yanking the knife handle from Lily's grasp. Lily went to lunge again, but the knife was deeply in. Smoke curled up from where the knife sat in the vampiress's back.

Lily watched, unable to tear her gaze away. In her mind's eye, she saw Xu Yu, grunting and screaming, flailing at his back, smoke curling from around the blade as he grew weaker and fell into a heap.

Wei Yen's death cries rang through the air. On her knees, she slumped over, staring at Lily with a nearly lifeless gaze. The glow of bloodlust had been extinguished, and her shoulders sagged. Without another sound, Wei Yen collapsed to the courtyard stones and lay completely still, Lily's knife protruding from her back.

Lily panted and stared. Her leg and back throbbed with pain. Blood poured from the bite wounds in her calf. Her clothing was shredded, and every muscle in her body screamed from the tension of combat.

She drew herself up into a kneeling position and sat, gasping for breath. Pain shot through her, and she fell over, her palms scraping on the stones. Wei Yen's body lay close by, emitting the odour of burnt rust.

Lily clenched her teeth against another wave of pain. She'd intended to pull her knife out but couldn't even lift her hand from the stone on which it rested.

*Wei Yen's...bite.* Lily had thought her system completely healed. Apparently not. Her weakened body couldn't withstand the poison of the vampiress' anger. Lily's mind fogged, but her body felt every lick of poison as it curled through her limbs, invaded her blood and internal organs. Her skin burned like a brand wherever Wei Yen had clawed or bitten her.

Lily's vision blurred, her hands on the stones became pale clouds. The blackness of night crowded in on her, pressing, and a sensation like the iron grip of hands on her throat cut off her air. Wei Yen was choking her? No. The vampiress lay dead. Lily clutched at her throat. No one choked her. She coughed, a spate of wracking convulsions that left her drained.

*Must...get...up.* She needed to get to her herbs before the poison choked the life out of her internal organs. If the toxins invaded the same part of her that could kill her if it were stabbed...

She pulled in a hard breath and focused, yanked every ounce of strength she had into her leg, to haul herself up. She managed to slide her foot out and plant it, sole down on the cobbles. Push, strain, fight—

A slice of pain threw her down. She landed on her stomach on the stones.

"Lily!"

The voice was familiar—male—pushing at the noxious fog enveloping her consciousness. Gentle hands slid underneath her and turned her onto her back. She blinked. The night sky above, dotted with stars...a face...hovering.

Tenzin?

"Lily, you've been poisoned. I must draw out the toxins."

She blinked. Her throat felt thick, as if someone had stuffed a rock into her gullet. A hand pushed her hair back, away from her neck.

"I'm going to feed on you," he said. Two emerald suns shone out from his face where his eyes should have been. "This is the only way, Lily. Forgive me."

He bent over her. The heat and darkness of his body covered her. She felt a sting on her neck and then pleasure, sheer pleasure.

The foggy darkness in her brain lightened from black to grey to milky white. A rhythmic tug on the side of her neck sent sparks of bliss cascading through her, as if an orgasm were erupting in every inch of her skin. Each pull of the sweet suction sent another wave of bliss, and she felt as if an invisible hole had opened somewhere inside her through which the poison and pain were draining away.

Her body was floating, inching upward, and Kwan Yin's golden face smiled down at her.

"*Tenzin*," Kwan Yin whispered. "*Tenzin*."

Lily smiled back at the goddess of compassion who continued to chant Tenzin's name in a caressing whisper.

Suddenly, the hot, delicious suction on her neck lifted. She almost cried out from the desolation the cool air on her skin left in its wake. She felt his warm tongue lick the same spot and then hands underneath her. Strong arms lifted her from the stones, and she was floating...no, being carried.

The spicy scent of a man—Tenzin—wafted around her languid body. She felt cleansed and sweetly sleepy as the rhythmic footsteps brought her out of the night air. The aroma of incense enveloped her, and she recognised the herbal scents of her bedchamber.

He lowered her down, and the softness of her bedding met her back. "Rest now, Lily," she heard him say. The covers came up over her, and she felt his energy around her, beside her. He was holding her hand between both of his.

*Don't leave, Tenzin.* She wanted to say the words but couldn't speak. The bliss she felt made speech impossible.

"I won't leave you, Lily. I'm here." He was leaning over, his face hovering within her range of vision. A faint smile curved his lips, and he reached out, smoothing a gentle hand over her brow.

Lily blinked, staring up at him. Had he heard her thought? Perhaps. He could also have sensed what she was feeling because they'd been in Heaven together. Surely their communion in front of Kwan Yin herself had bound their souls together.

She sighed and let her eyelids flutter closed. Tenzin's caress on her brow was relaxing her, like a potent infusion of sleeping herbs...

Tenzin's heart thudded as he watched Lily fall asleep. His beautiful Tigress. He brushed the pad of his thumb back and forth across her cheekbone. In spite of her illness, her skin was still soft and firm to his touch. He'd missed touching her so, even though it not been long since they'd made love.

He forced himself to lift his hand away. Let her rest now. Once the sedative effect of the feeding wore off, she would be stiff and sore from the aftereffects of the vampire's poison. Not to mention the emotional effects she'd feel. No doubt, centuries of hatred had built up in the vengeful vampiress and had poisoned Lily through her bites and scratches. He remembered his own depression after his sire had brought him across. In spite of how pleasurable the feeding had been, the vampire's turbulent emotions, lusts, hatreds and loves...all had entered Tenzin, and it had taken him a long time to process them all.

A cold prickle of forewarning skittered through his veins. What would Lily have to say when she woke up and realised he'd fed on her? Even though he'd done it to save her life, she was a strong-minded woman who associated vampire feeding with nightmarish pain and violation. He'd slipped up when he'd spoken to her after hearing the mind link they now shared. He'd just been so grateful and joyous that she'd not wanted him to leave. He'd have to be careful and ease into telling her of this new bond they shared. It was one thing to have their souls joined, as had happened in Heaven. But the physical links of their minds? How would she feel about that?

He sighed. Well, if that was the case, he'd handle it. Whether Lily wanted it or not, she was his soul mate. It was just better for both of them if she *wanted* it.

Her delicate hand still lay between both of his. It was barely midnight, but he didn't dare leave her to go and tell Fen Chow and the women in Plum House that the danger had passed. At least, he believed it had passed. He'd told them to wait until sunrise before venturing to return to the compound.

Which was yet another thing Lily might be furious about. She expected her Tigresses to be in Foshan by now. She'd been too exhausted and ill to realise he was with her, because they hadn't gotten on a train. When she woke up, her mind would probably be more alert.

Oh, well, he'd handle that too.

* * * *

"Tenzin."

Tenzin blinked. He raised his head from its resting place on his arms at the foot of the bed. Damn, he hadn't meant to fall asleep.

Lily's eyes were open.

He sat bolt upright and rose up on his knees.

Their gazes met.

"Tenzin." Her voice was nearly a whisper. Her raven hair was spread across her pillow, and her pale smooth skin was chalky. She looked nearly drained of life, but a faint smile touched her soft lips.

She blinked again.

A soft rustling carried from the doorway. Tenzin turned and saw Jade. Jade's eyes were locked hopefully onto Lily.

"She's awake," Tenzin said.

Jade's bruised face broke into a huge smile and her eyes immediately misted. She rushed over and knelt down. "Mistress Lily."

Lily's gaze shifted, and she blinked again. "Jade." Her eyes darted in Tenzin's direction and back to Jade. "You are supposed to be in Foshan."

Jade picked up Lily's hand. "Forgive me, Mistress Lily." She held Lily's hand up to her cheek, and Tenzin admired Jade's courage. "I begged Tenzin to let us stay nearby. I couldn't bear to leave you alone. Please, I beg you, don't be angry with him. He kept his promise. He made sure we were safe in Plum House. He stayed with us the whole time until he went to check on you. We were disobedient, all of us. We would have defied him no matter what."

Lily sighed. The expression on her drawn features was unreadable.

"Now," Jade said, letting Lily's hand down gently onto the bed, "you must have a bath and then healing."

Tenzin's heart thumped. "Should I leave?"

To his surprise, Jade turned to him. "You're her Jade Dragon, aren't you?"

He shook his head. "No, but I would wish to be."

Jade bowed her head. "I'm sorry, though I'm certain that the *yang* of your presence would stimulate Mistress Lily's healing centres." She looked hopefully down at Lily. "Wouldn't it, Mistress Lily?"

Lily closed her eyes. Had Jade meant to corner her this way? All night Lily had dreamed of Tenzin's fangs in her neck, sipping her blood. Indeed, this was what Tenzin had done when he found her collapsed in the courtyard. She'd been fed on too many times not to realise what was happening to her, even though she'd been nearly unconscious.

No, she wasn't angry at him, not for feeding on her. He'd saved her life, however joyless that life had been for a very long time. Her anger was at the injustice of the cold-blooded murder of Fei Liu, someone she'd loved dearly. In between her dreams of Tenzin's fangs in her flesh had been Fei Liu's screams and blood-soaked body.

Lily *was* furious at Tenzin, at Fen Chow, and at her Tigresses. They had all defied her wishes, and they all could have been at risk from Wei Yen's wrath. Who even knew if Wei Yen had minions, other lovers like the one who'd killed Fei Liu who would come to avenge the vampiress's death?

Had Lily the strength, she would have told them all this. She knew Tenzin's mind was linked to hers, and yet she didn't even have the strength to convey all these feelings to him in her thoughts.

Jade's hopeful gaze was still on hers. The Tigress's expectancy filled the air. Jade had been through horror herself lately, and Lily didn't wish to disappoint her. Nor did Lily exactly mind the prospect of Tenzin's company while she had a bath. In spite of their disobedience and the danger and her pains and aches, both physically and mentally, the constant comfort had been his presence.

"Of course, Jade," she managed to whisper.

A new, radiant smile broke out on Jade's face, a smile that went far to soften the bruises and cuts on the Tigress's cheeks and jaw, and Lily was glad she'd put aside her own anger.

"Tenzin can undress you while I heat some water." Jade rose and hurried from the room.

Tenzin felt a nervous tremor. Somehow this moment seemed to be one of reckoning. He'd watched a stream of thoughts and emotions pass through Lily's eyes, but she hadn't communicated any of them. "Lily, if you don't wish me to un--"

*"Tenzin, do it, please."*

His breath hitched softly. She knew about their mind link! He studied her eyes a moment as if he could decipher her feelings. Her gaze was steady, yet not readable. Trembling at the thought of seeing her beauty revealed again, he fumbled with the frog closures of her blouse. The tattered material fell open, revealing the soft white diamond of cloth at the front of her binding. He felt around the material for the ties.

*"I think it's best you cut the material off of me. It hurts too much to move."*

"Yes, you're right," he murmured.

*There's a small pair of shears in that box over there.* She indicated with a brief nod, and Tenzin saw an ornately carved box on a dresser in the corner. He retrieved the shears from it and returned to Lily's bedside. There seemed to be a natural flow to the communication through their mind link.

Very carefully, he cut up the length of the binding. The delicate cloth fell away, and Lily's breasts sprang free.

Tenzin stared at the luscious swells. Lily's dark nipples had already tightened, perhaps a response to the cool air hitting her skin. He felt his cheeks tingle and bowed his head. When he ventured a glance at Lily's face, he saw her pale cheeks had coloured.

*"I feel like such a fool, Tenzin. After everything we've done together, now I blush like a virgin."*

He chuckled, tension broken. "I understand." Reaching out, he brushed his fingertips across one of her pale cheeks. The silkiness of her skin weakened him. He felt his cock stir in his trousers.

*"Tenzin."* Her voice was a whisper in his mind.

Her eyes appeared misted over. A teardrop spilled from one eye and ran down her cheek.

"Lily, you're so beautiful." Unable to stop himself, Tenzin leant down and pressed his lips to hers. Though slightly dry, Lily's lips were still petal soft and tasted delicious. He closed his eyes, absorbed in the feel of her, and slipped his tongue gently past the seam of her lips, caressing her tongue with his. She murmured and parted her lips in obvious surrender. Her fingers still curled around his, and squeezed his hand.

"Oh, I'm sorry." Jade's voice broke the spell.

Tenzin sat up.

"I'll come back," Jade said.

"No." Lily's voice was soft and hoarse. Tenzin reached for a glass of water and helped her sip.

Jade proceeded in with a bowl of steaming water. "We must finish undressing her," Jade said.

He nodded and pulled Lily's shoes off. Jade undid Lily's pants, and Tenzin slipped them down her legs. Doing so released Lily's musky scent into the air, and he felt his cock respond. He appraised Lily's pale body, relieved to see that the bite marks and scratches had sealed up, leaving only the clear, silky skin that made his mouth water.

Jade dipped a cloth in the water, wrung it out, and wiped it across Lily's brow. "I see that Tenzin's *yang* has already begun your healing," she said. "Please forgive me. I know it's not my place to speak this way.

You may punish me later, if you wish. I was the wicked girl who fomented the rebellion against your wishes."

Tenzin saw Lily's face break into a faint smile. A bit of light infused her eyes. Her glance darted in his direction then back to Jade.

"Mistress Lily, I'm just so grateful to you," the Tigress went on. "I couldn't leave you. You don't understand the depths to which you have helped my life. All our lives." Jade paused in her speech, wet the cloth again, and bathed Lily's neck. "I know it's been a sore point for you that there have been no men to train as Jade Dragons. They are useless, so many of them. They either care about money or social status, not love and truth. But Fen Chow has asked to be my Jade Dragon. I believe he could be wonderful. Don't you? I told him I'd speak to you when you were well."

The smile on Lily's face deepened.

Suddenly Jade turned to Tenzin and extended the cloth. Her cheeks coloured a bit under the fading bruises. "I think that it's best you finish her bath," she said softly then dipped her head. "And then I will guide you in the healing sounds to give her. To strengthen her *yin*."

He took the cloth from Jade. "Of course."

Jade smiled. She bowed and knelt down with a gesture for him to bathe her mistress.

Tenzin dipped the cloth and wrung it out as he'd seen Jade do. He ran the cloth down Lily's arms then lifted one wrist to wash the soft recess of her underarm. His cheeks warmed, and his cock twitched. He could feel it stretching and hardening with each passing second of his fingers' contact with Lily's bare skin.

Her breasts rose and fell with her breathing, and he swore he could hear each breath deepen the longer he bathed her.

He wet the cloth some more and swirled it gently down her chest and around each breast. She sighed, and her eyelids fluttered as he brushed the soft cloth over the dark tips. The water left a glistening sheen on her satiny skin and darkened the ink of the leaping tiger as he moved the cloth over Lily's belly and ribcage.

With a tender lick, he covered the front of her sex, inching the cloth towards the tiger's belly. Small, dark hairs sprouted over her mound, which had always been bare, threatening to cover the inked skin. The sight roused Tenzin's desire, and he longed only to taste the moist crevice between her thighs.

Gently, he took hold of one thigh and moved Lily's leg aside. He wet the cloth and brushed it down the length of her slit.

She pulled in a breath, and her lips parted on the force of it. Her eyelids fluttered, and her hand clenched the bedding.

"Her *yin* is roused," Jade said in a gentle voice. "Now is the time to use the healing sounds. It is not difficult. Put your lips over her *yin* points, one at a time, and hum, very softly, in a continuous sound. This will stimulate her healing *yin*. You may begin with her mouth."

Tenzin's cheeks tingled madly at the thought of putting his mouth on Lily's body in front of Jade, but all that mattered to him was Lily's healing. He leant over and covered her mouth with his.

He caressed her hair back off her face and kept his lips over hers. Slowly he rested there and hummed, slowly, deeply, in a gentle rhythm into her mouth. As a monk, he'd spent many hours chanting in meditation. This, of course, was vastly different, but as the seconds passed, he felt their energies mingle.

Lily sighed again, a soft vibration that tickled his lips pleasantly. She touched the tip of her tongue to his, and Tenzin sensed the strength that seeped back into her. He answered the tiny movement in a soft dance of tasting the moist recesses of her mouth as he hummed, his breath mingling with hers.

"Now," Jade's voice drifted into the swirl of energy, "hum against her breasts, first one, then the other."

A tickle of excitement stirred in Tenzin's gut. He lifted his lips from Lily's. Hers remained parted, and she looked up at him, eyes wide and wondrous. The light of life burned in them for the first time since she'd opened them that morning.

He lowered himself down and bent over one breast. The soft mound beckoned to him with its pale beauty and dark, erect tip. Without hesitation, he covered it with his parted lips and resumed the gentle hum.

Lily's breathing deepened. Her breast bobbed against his mouth with her rising breaths. He felt one small hand on his head.

"Tenzin," she whispered.

Through the vibration, he heard her. Joy surged in him at her growing strength. He dared to brush the tip of his tongue across her nipple before lifting his mouth and tending to her other breast with the healing sounds.

A long time seemed to pass before Tenzin heard Jade's voice again.

"Now, bring your healing sounds to her jade cave."

Tenzin groaned against Lily's breast. That deep hidden part of her, musky and moist, that brought him so much pleasure, tasted so delicious he could barely contain himself. He lingered a moment on her breast and feathered the tip of his tongue on the hardened bud before lifting his face. He glanced to the side just in time to see Jade disappear through the doorway.

Lily moaned softly. The ecstatic sound pulled him back, and he climbed on the foot of the bed, kneeling between her firm, supple thighs. Her glistening *yin* petals were already partly opened. He pushed his thumbs into the moist folds and spread them. Her *yin* scent assaulted him, making him wondrously dizzy. He leant over and closed his lips over her musky inner sex.

Lily sighed and pushed her hips against his hands, a tiny movement that indicated the further strengthening of her *qi*.

His cock brushed against the bedding through his trousers as he sank down on his stomach between her thighs. Closing his eyes, he hummed against the moist warmth of her jade gate. Her scent and taste were so intoxicating, no herb or spice could compare. Again, he dared to venture the tip of his tongue against her *yin* pearl. Her breath caught, and her hand clutched at his head.

Lily gasped and her supple thighs fell further open. "Tenzin." She whispered his name several times, her head tilted back, breasts heaving with arousal. Her *yin* juices seeped generously onto his fingertips, showing him that she was already wanting him to fill her.

"Take me," she whispered.

Her fevered plea sent a shudder of arousal through him. He whipped his head up, feeling her *yin* dew lathered on his chin. "Lily, are you certain?" Such a chance was one he'd thought never to experience again, and his body trembled with need.

"Yes!"

He couldn't help the grin that spread across his lips, filled his entire being. Lifting himself to his feet, careful not to hurt her, he stripped off his clothing. At the last second, he remembered not to climb right on top of her and slide in. Just because her desire was as urgent as his was no reason to forget himself.

He leant over, braced himself on the mattress with one knee and slid one finger inside her. She moaned softly and arched her back. He sensed her silent demand for more and answered it. Pushing a second finger inside her slippery cave, he slid both fingers in and out in a gentle rhythm.

Lily thrashed her head back and forth on the pillow, whispering his name feverishly. The gathering energy of her life force pulsated into the air. The musky, sexual scent of her *yin* dew continued to pulse out into the air, and her nipples were still puckered into dark tips. Her pale skin was flushed now with a bit more colour, and her small delicate hands clutched the bedclothes.

His hunger surged. In one swift but gentle movement, Tenzin climbed on the bed and lowered his body carefully onto Lily's. He sank gently onto her softness, felt her firm breasts flatten deliciously against her chest, and his hard cock sought out the juncture of her legs.

Lily pulled her legs around his hips, giving him access to nestle in the slit of her sex. The head of his cock nudged her slick opening and he groaned as tingling pleasure flooded his entire lower region.

Bracing his upper body on his elbows, he gazed into her eyes. Their faces were so close together now that her warm breath caressed his lips. Her scent swirled in the air around them.

"Tenzin," she whispered. She wrapped her arms around him, and her fingertips pressed into his back. Her dark eyes appeared liquid, brimming with more unshed tears. "I love you."

The admission took his breath away. "I love you too." He pressed his lips to hers, kissed her tenderly, with every drop of feeling he had for her. With a gentle lick, he coaxed her lips apart, caressed the fullness of her lower lip and the most heat of her tongue.

She sighed into their joined mouths, and he felt her surrender the way she had the other morning, that glorious sweet moment when she'd opened her petals and let him sink deep inside her. That same liquid softness, the sweet spice of love he'd craved for centuries now, surrounded him in her feminine warmth and musky depth.

She shifted slightly underneath him, causing the head of his cock to sink in a bit deeper The pleasure tingled up his shaft and tightened his *yang* sac. He groaned and pushed with his hips, sheathing his stalk more than halfway.

Lily's fingers pressed into his back. She panted into his mouth and moaned softly. He thrust his hips gently, part teasing, part making sure she still wanted this.

A smile played about her lips, and she pushed against him. A glitter came into her eyes, and she surged underneath him. He gasped as her jade cave swallowed every inch of his cock in melting, wet, warm...

He groaned and took her lips in a hot kiss.

The world around Lily faded away. Tenzin's hard length deep inside her sent waves of pleasure through her entire sex. Her body melted into the union. The shaft of his dragon grazed her *yin* pearl with each slide of their bodies together. She gripped his back and closed her eyes, dancing her tongue against his. His male scent, musky and powerful, enveloped her as potently as the push of his thick, hard dragon stretching her, filling her.

"Yes," she whispered. Behind her eyelids, she saw the floating depths of Heaven.

The sound sent a palpable shiver of energy through Tenzin's body. Lily felt his hard muscles quiver under her hands. He deepened their kiss, his lips chafing hers hotly, tongue caressing hers in feral strokes.

Tenzin reached up and smoothed Lily's hair back, felt the warmth of life that had crept back into her skin. He pulled his lips from hers and gazed down at her. "Is this all right, Lily? He breathed. "Me inside you?"

She nodded, eyelids heavy over her dusky almond-shaped eyes. Her full lips were parted with her heavy breathing and pink coloured her cheeks warmly. "Yes, Tenzin. Yes."

Her enjoyment urged him on. He dipped his mouth to hers and captured her lips again. The movement made his cock slide inside her. The friction sent a blast of heat through him, and he started to move inside her again, long, easy strokes that made her moan softly into his mouth.

*"Tenzin."*

He peered down into her eyes. *"What is it, Lily?"*

*"Feed on me again, please."*

The mere request made his fangs start to itch and tingle. His body raged with unfulfilled need and the hunger to sip Lily's blood. "Are you sure? I can't believe--"

"Yes. Please, help me not be afraid." She locked her gaze with his. To his delight, hunger glazed her dark irises. Without a word, she tilted her head back.

The tiny movement sent the musky sweet smell of her flesh to his nostrils. He lowered his lips to the tender skin on the side of Lily's throat. Hunger ripped through him, raw and potent. He nuzzled the spot and felt Lily writhe against him. She squeezed her vaginal muscles around his cock, a silent demand that made him mindless.

He licked the spot he needed to puncture, curled his lips back, and sank his tingling incisors into Lily's flesh.

Lily's body jumped underneath him, and she gripped his back muscles. She released a long sigh and then sank down into the mattress as he pushed his fangs into her skin as deeply as they'd go.

He groaned softly. No one had ever tasted so honeyed, so potently delicious, as Lily. Perhaps she had the same flavour as any immortal woman, but to him, she was succulent, beautiful, and wondrous.

Because he loved her.

Slowly, carefully, he slid his fangs from her skin and closed his lips over the punctures. Lily sighed again and slid her hands down his back to his hips. The tiny feel of her warm hands clutching his hips, so close to his sensitive buttocks caused a surge of need and he began to suckle.

Gently, in long even sips, he drew out her blood. With each tug of his lips on her neck, he slid his jade stalk deep inside her.

Lily moaned again and squeezed Tenzin's hips. Pleasure flooded every inch of her body. She could never have imagined that being fed upon could feel like tiny orgasms exploding all over the surface of her skin. Sheer, utter, unfathomable bliss.

She tilted her head back even more, offering herself fully to Tenzin's suckling lips.

"Tenzin," she whispered again, as if uttering his name out loud sealed their bodies and souls together even more than this intimate act.

Her eyelids fluttered from the pleasure, and she could feel the last of Wei Yen's poison drain from her body. Tenzin surged against her, and his dragon grazed her yin pearl. Back and forth, he rubbed her sweet spot until the sensation of orgasm all over her body spread into her womb. The waves of bliss shuddered through her, melting away space and time. The pleasure wrung her clean, and she wilted underneath Tenzin's weight, her hands resting on his hard buttocks.

He lifted his lips from her neck and gently licked the punctures. Lily smiled and stared up at the ceiling. For the first time in her existence, she felt cleansed, peaceful, happy. Loved.

Tenzin caressed her hair as he gazed down at her. After several moments, a smile curved his lips.

She returned his smile. Tingling energy spiralled through her limbs, energy she hadn't felt in so long. She slid her hands over his arm muscles.

A silent moment passed and Lily became aware again of Tenzin inside her, his dragon still swollen and unfulfilled. She squeezed her muscles around him and moved her hips.

He sucked in a breath, and his golden skin darkened. "Take your pleasure, my love," she whispered. She bucked her hips again, and Tenzin took her lips in a hot kiss. Bracing his weight on his elbows, he thrust inside her again, in long, delicious strokes that massaged her inner walls and brought her to another blissful explosion.

In moments, Tenzin stiffened. With his mouth locked over hers, he stopped moving. Lily felt the warm gush of his *yang* cloud inside her womb. As his body relaxed, he kissed her softly before pulling back and gazing at her. His long lashes were heavy over his dusky eyes.

Lily reached up and touched his damp cheek. A sudden surge of shame reddened her cheeks. "Tenzin, I have to tell you something."

"Yes?"

"You are already my Jade Dragon." She smiled and kissed his parted lips. "Don't you understand what a Jade Dragon is? He's a man who supports a Tigress's spiritual work, who protects her, and is there for her. Aside from the physical skills of retaining your *yang*, you have already done these things and more."

Those incredible eyes misted. "I'm honoured." He clasped his hand over hers and pressed his lips into her palm. He slipped out of her and gathered her against him.

She settled into the warm strength of Tenzin's body. She smiled again, flooded by a sense of contentment she'd never known. "Thank you, Tenzin."

Tenzin's hand moved gently over her hair. "I'm sorry I disobeyed you, Lily. In my place, you would have taken the women to Foshan, I'm certain."

"What you did was far more noble." She kissed him again. "You did the right thing. You did what a true friend would have done."

He stared down at her his amber eyes misted. "Friend?"

Warmth flooded Lily's body. When she'd first seen Tenzin on the platform in the gaming parlour, his perfect attitude and abundant life force had made him seem to be a living, breathing ace in the hole for her

Tigress practice. How wrong she'd been. He was more. So much more. She smiled and snuggled in closer to him. To the man she loved. "Yes," she said softly. "Friend. Best friend."

# About the Author

Sedonia Guillone is a multi-published, award nominated author of both m/f and m/m erotic romance. The man in her life is her inspiration and provides all the hands-on research she needs. When she's not writing, she's cuddling, watching samurai flicks and thinking about the next naughty, delicious tale she wants to write.

Sedonia loves to hear from readers. You can find her contact information, website details and author profile page at http://www.total-e-bound.com.

# Total-E-Bound Publishing

www.total-e-bound.com

Take a look at our exciting range of literagasmic™
erotic romance titles and discover pure quality
at Total-E-Bound.